THE MINISTER IS MURDERED

A HUMOROUS PARANORMAL COZY MYSTERY

CARLY WINTER

Edited by
DIVAS AT WORK EDITING
Cover by
COVEREDBYMELINDA.COM

WESTWARD PUBLISHING / CARLY FALL, LLC

Copyright © 2021 by Carly Winter

All rights reserved.

No part of this book may be reproduced in any form or by any electronic or mechanical means, including information storage and retrieval systems, without written permission from the author, except for the use of brief quotations in a book review.

This is a work of fiction. Unless otherwise indicated, all the names, characters, businesses, places, events and incidents in this book are either the product of the author's imagination or used in a fictitious manner. Any resemblance to actual persons, living or dead, or actual events is purely coincidental.

Cover by: CoveredbyMelinda.com

THE MINISTER IS MURDERED

Be careful what you wish for... it may come true.

When Bernie, Adam and their friends travel to the idyllic town of Heywood, Arizona, to witness a marriage, they never expected to find the officiating minister poisoned to death.

With the Heywood sheriff being a novice to murder cases, she enlists Adam's help, and Ruby and Bernie decide to launch their own side investigation. Yet, with a near-death experience and a town populated by questionable residents with deep secrets, the killer remains elusive.

A series of explosive events will change Bernie and Ruby relationship forever... if they can catch the killer before he gets to Bernie first.

CHAPTER 1

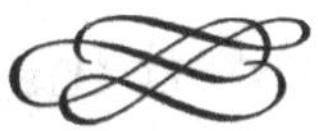

LARGE, gallant spruce and fir trees sandwiched the two-lane road while the sun shone brightly above. I held Adam's hand as he drove. My SUV hummed along quietly on our way to Heywood, the town my friend, Darla, had chosen for her wedding.

It should have been a nice experience. Maybe even romantic. Except, we had my ghostly grandmother in the back seat.

"Are we there yet?" she whined for what seemed like the hundredth time. I'd lost track and my patience was wearing thin.

"No. Quit asking me that," I grumbled. "We're there when the car stops."

Adam chuckled and shook his head while I

admired his square jawline and the cute curl of blond hair just above his ear.

"This is taking forever!" Ruby complained.

"You sound like a toddler, not a dead woman. Dead people don't whine."

She muttered something about me being a party pooper and lay down on the backseat with her feet up against the window. A lecture on seatbelt safety sat on the tip of my tongue, but I held it. She could fly through the windshield without so much as a scratch.

But honestly, she was right—the drive to the Arizona-Colorado border seemed to be taking a long time. I'd debated asking Adam if he was lost. Glancing at my phone, I noted I still didn't have any service so I couldn't map out our location. Instead, I closed my eyes, determined to nap until we arrived.

A few moments later, Adam slowed, and dirt crunched under the tires. I glanced up to find him pulling over.

"Take a look at that," he whispered.

I gasped as I stared at the town below.

"That looks nice," Ruby said. "Very rustic. It reminds me of those Hallmark movies you like to watch."

Built on a winding river surrounded by

forests, it did resemble something one would find in a Hallmark Christmas movie. Immediately, my mood perked up and I couldn't wait to explore the quaint, seemingly magical place.

As we descended, the forest once again swallowed us up until we emerged onto the main road through town. On the left, the heavy foliage remained. To the right stood the storefronts, and behind them, the river. People milled about, window shopping and going on with their days.

I glanced at my phone. We still had almost an hour before we needed to meet Darla at the church. "Let's park and walk around," I said. "Maybe grab some lunch?"

"Sounds great," Adam murmured. "Looks like there's a spot right in front of the ice cream store."

"What's the Scoop?" Ruby snickered. "What a cute business name!"

The line out the front also indicated they offered excellent product.

After parking, we exited the car and I reached my hands above my head and stretched. The sun warmed my face as I inhaled the fresh, mountain air. How had I never known about Heywood?

Adam took my hand and we strolled down the sidewalk passing a gift shop, a hunting and fishing store, and a doctor's office. Ruby spun around in circles next to me, her purple muumuu flaring around her thin legs.

"I bet nothing bad ever happens here," she said. "This place is perfect. Not even a speck of garbage on the street."

"Are you hungry?" Adam asked. We stopped at a restaurant aptly named On the River. "Do you want to eat now or wait a bit?"

My stomach growled as the smell of grilled burgers wafted our way. "Now would be good."

As we opened the door and strolled in, the heavy wooden floorboards creaked under our feet and the log walls had been decorated with scenic photos of the river and forest, and its inhabitants. A picture of a bear walking the shore with two cubs trailing behind her caught my eye.

"Oh, that mama doesn't look happy," Ruby said. "She's probably had it with the two cubs. You can see all she wants is to lie down and have someone get her a fish or some garbage to eat."

"You can tell all that by the picture?" I asked, smiling. "Are you the bear whisperer now?"

She shrugged. "Just trying to put myself in her place. If I were her, I'd run for the hills and leave those two little turds to fend for themselves."

"No, you wouldn't."

"Maybe, maybe not. We'll never know."

"Can I help you?" I turned to find a server approaching. About my height but maybe a couple of years younger, her rosy cheeks glowed with health when she smiled. Must have been all the clean, fresh, mountain air.

"We'd like to grab some lunch," Adam said.

"Two of you?"

"No, three," I replied without thinking.

She furrowed her brow in confusion as she glanced around. "Are they meeting you later?"

Dang it. "I'm sorry. I meant two of us," I said as my face burned with embarrassment. Sometimes, I forgot no one could see Ruby but me.

The server smiled wider. "It's a beautiful day. Would you like to eat outside?"

"As long as we don't see any bears," Ruby muttered, but I wasn't sure why she cared. She was already dead.

"That sounds great," Adam replied. "Thank you."

We followed her through the restaurant to the expansive outdoor deck. With a gasp, I took in the beauty.

The river shore lay about two hundred feet away and the sound of the meandering water met my ears as a breeze whispered through the trees.

On the River was a busy place and I counted ten full tables on the deck. As we were led to our seats, I studied the other guests' food. Club sandwiches, a stacked burger, a beautiful salad... was that a chocolate cake? My mouth watered while I sat down.

"Can I get you two started with something to drink?"

Leaning over the table conspiratorially, Adam asked, "Do you want some wine?"

"It's only one in the afternoon!"

"Oh, for the love of everything holy, Bernie!" Ruby yelled. "Look at the place! Have a glass of wine and enjoy it!"

I shot Ruby a glare, then nodded. While Adam ordered a bottle, I glanced over the menu, but that salad I'd seen on the way in had caught my eye.

A few moments later, the server returned and poured us each a glass. "Are you two in town for something special, or just passing through?"

"A wedding," I replied. "Our friends are getting married this weekend."

"How nice," she said, setting down the bottle and pointing to her left. "The church is up around the bend. Beautiful place. Also, if you have time, make sure you check out the Farmers' Market, which is just a little farther past the church. It runs Tuesdays and Saturdays until four and features local businesses and artists."

"Thank you," Adam said. "We'll definitely head over."

I sipped my wine and took in the stunning views. Across the river, a fisherman emerged from the trees and began casting while people floated past us in tubes and rafts. Ruby stretched out on the deck next to the table just as my cranky cat, Elvira, would do at home, basking in a ray of sunshine. "I'm just going to lie here and pretend I can feel the sun on my face and breathe in all this fresh air."

Adam and I planned the rest of our afternoon over our salads. We'd have a little time to hit the Farmers' Market and then head over to the church to meet Darla and Jack. Instead of driving, we decided to walk the Riverwalk, which stretched as far as we could see.

An hour later, the three of us strolled through the market but the views kept grabbing my attention away from the goods being offered. A woman who I thought I recognized caught my eye and I beelined it over to her booth, Sage Advice.

She smiled broadly when I approached and I

swore I knew her from somewhere. In her fifties, black and gray curly hair framed her thin face, little lines appearing around her eyes as she grinned. "Can I help you?"

I glanced at her product. Soap and bath bomb baskets, tinctures, and teas for everything from anxiety to Valley Fever. A vanilla scent tickled my nose and I picked up a small basket of bath bombs.

"Those also contain some chamomile for relaxation," she said.

"They smell amazing."

"Thank you. I thought so too."

"Do you make all this yourself?"

She nodded. "Well, I help make them. My boss is the real herbal wizard."

As I brought the cellophaned package to my nose, I inhaled deeply. So good.

"We know her from somewhere," Ruby said. I glanced over to find her staring at the woman, her lips pinched in concentration. "I just can't place from where."

I fully agreed but decided to allow the matter to rest. Yes, she did look familiar, but saying that to a stranger always seemed to lead to awkward conversations while both parties tried to figure it all out. I handed the woman the bath bomb basket. "I'll take this."

"You're going to love it," she said, slipping it into a paper bag. "These are my absolute favorites for relaxation. Put on some soft music and pour a nice glass of merlot, and you'll feel so much better."

"Well then, take my money!" I shoved my bills at her.

She threw her head back and laughed. "Gladly! Thank you and enjoy your bath bombs."

"Where do we know her from?" Ruby asked as we left the booth.

"I'm not sure," I whispered.

"That's the mystery we're going to solve while we're here!" Ruby shouted as she jumped up and down. "Let's figure that out!"

I nodded and smiled as Adam stopped to check out the local hot sauce vendor, Too Hot to Handle.

"Oh, look!" Ruby squealed. "I need one of their t-shirts! It describes me perfectly."

"Not sure about that. Maybe it should read, too cold to care," I muttered under my breath as Adam shoved a cracker in his mouth and his face quickly turned bright red.

"I like that one, too," Ruby said, snickering. "I am dead, and I don't care about much."

As Adam asked for a glass of water, I turned back to Sage Advice and eyed the woman once again. Indeed, maybe that should be the mystery to be solved. As Ruby had said, nothing bad would ever happen in this beautiful utopia.

My phone rang and I pulled it from my pocket. Darla.

"Are you here?" she asked breathlessly.

"Yes. It's beautiful."

She squealed. "Wait until you see the church!"

"Are you there now?"

"Almost. Maybe ten minutes?"

"We're right down the street, so we'll meet you then."

I turned and tapped Adam on the shoulder. His eyes watered as his cheeks reddened.

"I think I'm dying," he whispered while in the midst of a coughing fit. "The guy dared me to try the Devil's Juice."

Ruby roared with laughter as tears tracked down his cheeks. "He looks like his face is about to explode!"

"We have to go meet Darla, so get yourself together," I said, shaking my head. "Put that fire out."

"Oh, he's going to stink tonight!" Ruby chortled. "That stuff is going to do a number on his stomach!"

I rolled my eyes as the vendor chuckled and poured a glass of milk for my suffering boyfriend.

When his head no longer looked like it was about to burst, we strolled down the Riverwalk to the church. Another pathway led up to the front of it, which faced the street. I pulled on the large wooden door and was surprised to find it open.

"See?" Ruby said. "Nothing bad ever happens here or they wouldn't leave the doors open."

"That's not really safe," Adam muttered, his brow furrowed. "They should be locking the doors." Always the cop.

We went inside. Heavy silence blanketed the church. Wooden pews lined each side of the aisle while the red carpet muffled our footsteps. Stained glass windows cast beautiful rainbows. Behind the stone altar, floor-to-ceiling windows showcased the view of the river and the mountains behind it.

"What a pretty place to get married," I whispered, not wanting to disturb the tranquility.

"Sure is," Adam murmured.

"Churches usually give me the creeps," Ruby said. "But I like this one. It's homey, not pretentious."

We turned as the doors opened. Darla and Jack entered and she hurried down the aisle to give us hugs.

"Yoohoo! Hey there, Mr. Dimples!" Ruby called. "I have lots of things to say to you, but they probably shouldn't be uttered in a church!"

As she batted her eyelashes at Jack, I embraced Darla.

"Isn't it gorgeous?" she whispered. I nodded and she glanced around. "Where's the minister? He's supposed to meet us."

"We haven't seen anyone," I said, shrugging.

"Let's wait a few minutes," Jack suggested, placing his arm around Darla.

After taking a seat in a pew, we spoke in low tones about the town and the beauty of the surrounding area. Darla glanced at her phone, furrowing her brow. "We were supposed to meet fifteen minutes ago. Maybe we should go in back?"

"Give him a call first," Jack said. "He's most likely running late."

When no one answered, she stood and headed towards a doorway to the left of the altar. "Hello?" she called, then disappeared into the back of the church.

A moment later, she screamed.

CHAPTER 2

"WHAT THE HECK?" Jack sprang to his feet and sprinted down the aisle with Adam, Ruby, and me following close behind him. "Darla! Darla!" He rushed through the doorway. "Where are you?"

"Isn't Mr. Dimples cute when he gets all worried like that?" Ruby mused, seemingly not concerned about Darla in the least bit.

We found her kneeling in a small hallway, her hands covering her mouth while tears streamed down her cheeks. She pointed into a room to her right. "He's... he's blue," she whispered.

As Jack dropped to his knees and pulled Darla close to his chest, Adam and I glanced into the office. I assumed the dead man sitting behind the desk wearing a clerical collar was indeed the minister we were supposed to be meeting. And yes, he was blue.

A string of curses fell from Adam's lips as he stepped into the room pulling his phone from his pocket while I remained in the doorway. I knew better than to contaminate the scene. I surveyed the bookcases behind him lined with full rows of tomes. The red carpet needed replacing, or at least a really good cleaning. Light streamed in through the window and bounced off the eggshell walls, brightening the room. Ruby walked over to the minister and stared at him, nose-to-nose. "Sorry, big guy," she said. "What happened to you? Did you choke on that salad?"

I hadn't even noticed the Tupperware container sitting on the desk in front of him, mainly because I didn't want to look in his direction. The lettuce hadn't wilted, so if he had choked on the contents, it hadn't been too long ago.

While Adam felt for a pulse and spoke in low tones into the phone, Ruby continued to snoop around the body.

"Maybe you should step away from there," I said, pointing to her.

Of course, she ignored my suggestion. But really, what did it matter? She was a ghost and couldn't mess with evidence. Except she'd recently developed the ability to move inanimate objects. Dang it. "Ruby, please don't touch anything."

She rolled her eyes. "I'm not! Jeez, Bernie. Relax."

With no choice but to believe her—which I didn't—I shut my eyes for a moment so I didn't have to witness her ruin the scene.

"Bernie, do you think this is a murder or did he choke?" Ruby asked.

"I don't know," I muttered, trying not to study the minister's blue lips too carefully. I'd had experience with finding bodies with blue lips and nailbeds, and it meant a poisoning before. I didn't see why this would be any different. "We'll leave that up to the professionals." But in my heart, I knew I was standing in the middle of a murder scene because it happened to me so frequently.

By now, it shouldn't faze me. People around me were killed every few months, and somehow, I found myself involved in either solving the crime, or being accused of it. Neither position I considered a good time.

I turned toward the hallway to make sure Darla was okay. With her schizophrenia, I worried about her. Living her life was always such a delicate balance and anything could send her in the wrong direction. "Is she okay?" I asked as Jack met my gaze.

He nodded and pointed toward the office. "That's the guy who was supposed to marry us."

"I'm sure there's another minister around," I said. "We'll get it figured out." At least, I hoped we would. Darla had been so excited about her nuptials, and I didn't want anything to ruin her day… even death.

When I glanced back at the body, I yelped at finding Ruby standing right next to me. "Don't do that!" I sniped. "You know I hate it when you scare me like that!"

"I didn't mean to that time," she said. "That one's on you. Someone's a little jumpy."

Jumpy? Yes. Out of my skin jumpy. Finding dead people had that effect. I rubbed my sweaty hands on my jeans and hitched my purse up on my shoulder.

Adam returned to the doorway and pushed his phone into his jeans pocket. "The local sheriff is on her way."

"We need to find someone to marry Darla," I whispered. "She's so upset right now, and you know how I worry about her."

"They aren't going to be able to be married in the church until the police have finished their investigation," Adam murmured. "At this point, we don't know if it's choking, a heart attack, or a murder."

I sighed and shook my head. "Adam, we know it's a killing. His lips and nails are blue. He had to have been poisoned."

"Let forensics decide that, okay?" he said. "Let's not jump to conclusions."

Ruby rolled her eyes. "The only conclusion there is to jump to is that minister has been murdered. End of story."

Footsteps sounded from the church and all of us turned to find a thin, yet muscular woman in a green sheriff's uniform stroll in. In her fifties with short black hair framing her face, her mouth sat in a thin line of agitation. "Which one of you is Adam?"

All of us turned to him.

"Nice to meet you, Sheriff," he said, extending his hand. "Adam Gallagher."

"Mallory Richards. You can call me Mal."

After they shook hands, she glanced over his shoulder. "Is George in his office?"

Adam nodded and stepped out of her way.

Mal entered and stopped, placing her hands on her gun belt, slowly studying the scene. "Adam? Can you come here for a second?"

He hurried to her side. They spoke in hushed tones, making it difficult to hear. Ruby raced over and stood right behind them. Once again, I appreciated my ghost's ability to effortlessly eavesdrop, even if it was the wrong thing to do.

As they talked, Mal pointed around the room. After they finished their discussion, Adam returned to me while she jotted down her notes.

"What did she say?" I whispered.

"Thinks the holy one was offed," Ruby chimed in.

"She's considering it a murder scene until it can be proven otherwise," Adam said.

"Can all of you go wait out in the church?" Mallory asked. "But don't go anywhere. I need to get statements."

Jack helped Darla to her feet, and I followed them.

"Adam!" Mallory called. "Stay here a minute."

The two huddled together once more as Ruby skipped around me. "We've got another mystery to solve!"

"Another?" I asked.

"Yes! We've got to figure out where we know the bath bomb lady from and now, we have to crack the case of who murdered the minister."

I'd prefer to just go home. So much for our weekend in utopia.

Once Darla, Jack, and I were seated in the pew, we all stared at the altar. The air had changed. The once peaceful atmosphere had shifted into one of distress. Tears tracked down Darla's cheeks while Jack held her close. I took some deep breaths in the hopes of calming my racing heart.

Time passed slowly as I waited for Adam. When he finally took a seat next to me, I asked him what Mallory had said.

"She wants me to help out in the investigation," he said. "She's got a skeleton crew right now. A couple are away at training and the flu's going around. With her wanting to attempt to clear this within the first forty-eight hours, she needs all hands on deck."

And now I apparently wouldn't be heading home, either.

I attempted a smile. "I'm glad you can stick around to help her."

"I'm going to call Sheriff Walker," Adam said. "See if he can give her a hand for a day or two as well. It's been four years since there was a murder here, and Mallory's not happy about it."

"She's certain he was killed and didn't choke on a piece of lettuce?"

Adam nodded. "She's treating it as such until she has further evidence that it's not. All the clues point to him being poisoned."

"How? The salad?"

"There's a cup of coffee on his desk. She's thinking the poison was administered there."

"So, it had to be someone in his inner circle in order to get close to his coffee."

"The cup is from Cup of Go, the coffee shop in town. We'll have to trace his movements and see if he bought it there, or if someone brought it to him."

The church doors opened, casting a wide slice of sunlight down the aisle. A heavy woman in her sixties slowly walked toward us. As she came closer, I noted her hard blue eyes and gray pixie haircut. She didn't smile but narrowed her gaze on us.

"What are you kids doing in here?" she asked, her voice raspy like a heavy smokers'. Considering we were all approaching forty, I found her choice of words amusing.

"This one looks like Little Miss Sunshine," Ruby muttered. "I'm wondering who placed a turd in her cereal this morning."

"We… we were supposed to meet the minister today to discuss my friend's wedding this coming weekend," I said.

"Is that old coot running late again?" she asked, rolling her eyes. "That man wouldn't be on time even if he wore twelve watches."

"Actually, he's dead," Adam said. "I'm Deputy Adam Gallagher from Sedona."

Her eyes widened as she took his outstretched hand. "I'm Ethel. What do you mean George is dead?"

Adam cleared his throat and grinned. "Sheriff Mallory Richards is in back with him now."

Ethel sighed and took a seat. "Well, I'll be darned."

"Did you know him well?" I asked.

"We've been working together at the church for about three years. I spent six hours with him, five days a week. Knew him better than I knew my own sister."

"What do you do here?" Adam asked.

"I ran the administration. Paid the bills, kept his appointments, booked the church for weddings and funerals… kept the place running."

As she stared at the altar, I noted the lack of emotion.

"Shouldn't she be a little more upset?" Ruby

asked, sitting next to her. "Her co-worker is dead."

Agreed. But maybe she was in shock, or she simply didn't want to show her sadness in public.

"What was it?" Ethel asked. "Heart attack? I told him he needed to watch what he ate."

"The sheriff thinks he was murdered," Adam said.

She pursed her lips and nodded, still not fazed by the news. "That makes sense."

I traded glances with Adam and he furrowed his brow. "Why do you say that?"

"Because no good deed ever goes unpunished," Ethel said. "I told him that, too."

CHAPTER 3

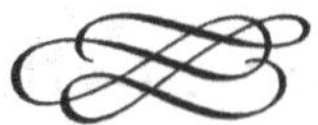

"WHAT DOES THAT MEAN?" Ruby asked. "Not that she's wrong. Doing good deeds all the time is a tough row to hoe."

"Would you care to elaborate?" Adam asked, lowering himself into the pew. I did the same and we both turned so we could face Ethel behind us.

"George was a decent guy," she said. "Maybe too nice. He was always bending over backwards to help others."

"What's wrong with that?" Adam asked.

"Well, in George's case, he became so hyper-focused on those he thought needed his help, he forgot about those close to him."

I traded glances with Adam, still not fully understanding what she was getting at.

"When he became a man of the cloth, he was married," Ethel continued. "His wife left him about a year ago, claiming she couldn't always be in second place."

"Can you start at the beginning?" Adam asked. "When did George come to the church?"

"About three years ago."

"And he was married?"

"Yes. He was in his forties when he finished seminary school. A late bloomer, if you will."

"Did they have any children?"

Ethel shook her head. "No. His ex-wife, Denise, told me they'd tried for years, but had never succeeded. George didn't want to go through any doctor to have kids and said if God wanted him to be a father, He'd bless them with a baby."

"That's too bad," I murmured. Adam shot me a glare, indicating I should keep my mouth shut.

Ethel continued, "Denise shared that George believed God didn't want him to be a father to one child, but to many. That's why he became a minister. It was his calling, and he was good at it."

Just then, Mallory strolled out from the back. "Ethel. Glad you're here. We're going to have to shut down the church for a bit. Do you want to grab anything from your office?"

Pursing her lips, she shook her head. "No. I've got everything I need."

"Excellent. The coroner is on his way and I told him to come in through the back door. Is there any problem with that?"

Ethel pulled out her phone from her purse and held it up. "We put one of those fancy doorbells back there, so I get a notification when someone comes around. The door sticks a bit when you try to open it from the outside, but a hard shove from the inside usually dislodges it."

I wondered if they also paid to keep the recordings of who came and went. If so, this could reveal some suspects.

"Do people usually come in through the back or in here through the church?" the sheriff asked.

"Depends," Ethel said, shrugging. "I hate leaving the church doors open, but George insisted people be allowed in to pray whenever the feeling struck. For a while, I demanded they be locked, especially when I was here alone, but he overrode me. Others' needs were greater than mine."

She brought the theme around again very quickly and I made a mental note to bring it up to Adam, although he had most likely caught it.

"Can you run us through your day?" the

sheriff asked, leaning against the pew and pulling out her notebook.

"Sure. I got here about nine and opened up. Then—"

"Which door did you use?" Mal asked.

"The church doors. I can't jimmy that one in back from the outside."

"Okay. Then what?"

"I put on a pot of coffee and listened to the voicemails and wrote everything down. George arrived about twenty minutes later. We chatted a bit about Tricia Yeats and—"

"Who's that?" Adam asked.

Ethel rolled her eyes. "Tricia is the biggest pain in my backside I've had in years. She wanted to get married this Saturday but—"

"That's the day I'm getting married!" Darla blurted.

We all turned to her and Jack sitting across the aisle. They'd been so quiet, I'd forgotten they were there.

"Well, Tricia wanted your day first. In fact, she had put in a reservation almost six months ago."

"What happened?" Mallory asked.

"George had promised her the church for the day and even put it on the calendar—*in ink*. But she never put down a deposit and the rule is, we don't write anything in ink unless we have the money in hand. This really upped my blood pressure. Months went by and every time I spoke to her, she promised she'd be in to write a check. One time she actually did give me one. Hallelujah, the girl had finally paid her bill. It bounced. From then on, I insisted she pay with cash."

"What about credit cards?" Adam asked.

"We don't take them. The fees are too high. We run a pretty lean budget here and every cent counts."

I also hated credit card fees, but I looked at them as the cost of doing business. I'd never survive if I didn't accept them, but perhaps a church ran differently than a bed and breakfast.

"Okay, let's come back to Tricia," the sheriff said. "I want to hear about the rest of your morning."

"Well, after our discussion, I went to my office and did some accounting, took a few calls and wrote some letters on George's behalf for him to sign later."

"Did anything seem out of the ordinary to you?" Mallory asked. "Did he have any visitors?"

Ethel shook her head. "Not that I recall. Just a regular morning. Although, I did hear him greet someone. I'm not sure if he was on the phone or if the person had come in. I just shut my office door in case I wasn't supposed to hear the conversation."

"Like what?" Adam asked.

"People come to him to confess their transgressions. We had a guy come in here and beg for forgiveness for stealing. Another confessed to cheating on his wife. I don't like to know who it is or what they say in case I see them around town. I'm better off being in the dark about people's secrets and sins. I'm no gossip."

I arched an eyebrow. No one had accused her of being one, which probably meant she was indeed a huge chinwagger. Perhaps what she'd meant was she didn't like to be aware of people's sins and secrets because then she had nothing to gossip about. Maybe she became wracked with guilt after spilling the tea.

"He had a cup from Cup of Go on his desk," Mallory said. "Did you bring that to him?"

"Pfft. Never stepped foot in the place. I can make my own coffee. Why in the world would I spend that much money on coffee?"

Because it's good? But she did have a point. It was a lot to spend on beans that could easily be ground up at home. Yet, I hadn't managed the art of designing my latte, and that was one of my favorite parts of buying an overpriced coffee. I appreciated the art.

"Do you know who did?" Adam asked.

Ethel shook her head. "No, I don't."

"When did you go to lunch?" Mallory questioned.

"At one."

The sheriff checked her phone. "Well, it's almost four. Are your lunches usually that long? Where have you been?"

"They are on days I visit my mother in the nursing home," Ethel said. "George and I had an agreement that I spend two afternoons a week with my mom because that's when she's most responsive. She's got Alzheimer's, and I like to see her when she has at least a vague idea of who I am. After three, she watches TV, has an early dinner, and conks out. She doesn't know her own name then, let alone mine."

"That woman must be close to two-hundred years old!" Ruby shouted. "How can this old bag have a living mother?!"

Ethel couldn't be older than her sixties. Of course, her mother could be living, but Ruby had always been worse at math than me. I'd explain it to her later.

"What days do you go?" Adam asked.

"Tuesdays and Fridays."

Of course, they'd verify her story. I rubbed my temples, wishing we could go home. The afternoon wine had fired up a headache. Or maybe it was the stress of being caught in another murder investigation.

Glancing over at Darla, I noted she was crying once again. "They need to leave," I said, elbowing Adam.

He nodded and turned to Mal. "Can you interview our friends? They need to get back to the bed and breakfast we're staying in. She's really upset."

"Of course." She pulled out an extra pad and pen from her breast pocket and handed them to Adam. "Please continue with Ethel here, and I'll take care of them."

"So, tell us about Tricia," Adam said while the sheriff approached Darla and Jack. "She had her wedding date booked, but she hadn't given you a deposit."

"She tried, but the check bounced," Ethel reminded him.

"What happened then?"

"I started to get inquiries about the date, so I took her off the calendar. I had to use whiteout to do it since George had noted her name with a pen, but I did it."

"She really finds it irritating he wrote on the calendar in ink," Ruby mused, grinning. "She'd never survive a day in my old life."

Ruby had probably never had a calendar, let alone worried about whether what she wrote down was in pencil or pen.

"What happened then?" Adam asked, scribbling notes as he spoke.

"Well, Darla over there came to see the church and immediately plunked down her deposit. I put *her* name in pen. George was angry."

"Why?"

Ethel shrugged. "Because he believed Tricia was a good girl and would eventually give us the deposit."

"How did Tricia find out she wouldn't be getting married here?" Adam asked.

"I called her. She begged and pleaded with me to keep the date and she would have the money soon."

"And then?"

"I told her no. We had paying people who wanted the date and they'd get it."

"What did she say to that?"

Ethel rolled her eyes and shook her head, her

mouth in a thin line of disgust before she answered. "Screamed at me like a crazy banshee. After a few minutes, I hung up on her."

Adam and I traded glances. "Was that the last you heard from her?" he asked.

"Oh, heck no. She called a few more times." Ethel crossed her arms over her chest and stared at the altar again. "I don't like to speak ill of people, but Tricia Yeats is the nastiest little thing this side of Phoenix. Always has been."

"Did she ever come to the church?" Adam asked.

"You mean for service?"

"Sure. Was she a regular here?"

"No. I'd never seen her before the whole wedding fiasco started."

"And what about after you pulled the date from her?" Adam asked. "Did she come to the church then?"

"Oh, yes. she showed up here, screaming and cursing like she'd just walked directly out of Satan's portal."

"What exactly did she say?" Adam asked.

"Told me I was a fat, old cow, begged George to let her have the date, promised him things... things young, unmarried women shouldn't be thinking about."

"Oh, I want to hear about those," Ruby said, leaning forward. "That sounds like my kind of discussion!"

Adam's cheeks had reddened, and I pursed my lips together to hide a smile. I could only imagine what was going through his mind. "Would you feel more comfortable talking about that with the sheriff?"

"Maybe, maybe not," she replied, shrugging.

"Was there anything else Tricia said that we should know about?" Adam asked.

"Yes. The last time she came in here there weren't any tears and sorrow. Instead, she was angrier than a snake disturbed while sunning itself."

"When was that?"

"Two days ago."

Adam scribbled in the notepad again. "What did she have to say?"

"She tossed a few chairs, did a lot of screaming and yelling, then threatened George that if he didn't hold the wedding on the day she wanted, she'd kill him."

CHAPTER 4

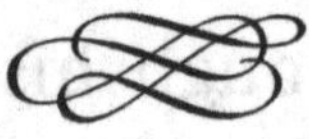

THE THING about owning a bed and breakfast was that it made me a terrible guest. I studied every detail when we pulled up. The gardenias needed watering and the railing on the staircase could use a bit of paint. I loved the doorbell chime, which almost sounded like a lullaby, as well as the two white rocking chairs on the porch. As the door opened, a woman about my age with long blonde hair greeted us with a warm smile, and I could only hope I seemed as friendly to my guests as she did.

"Welcome! Welcome!" she exclaimed, stepping aside. "I'm Mandy. The rest of your party is already here."

As I entered, my critique continued. Loved the

black leather overstuffed sofas in the living room, littered with ocean blue and yellow throw pillows, but she needed end tables. Why only a coffee table? Should I have taken off my shoes? The plush, taupe rug seemed like it would be difficult to keep clean. Hardwood was so much easier for upkeep. When I walked by a side table and found myself running a finger over it to check for dust, I silently cursed.

"You need to stop that," Ruby muttered. "Trust me. No one's home is as clean as yours. You've set the bar too high for the rest of the mere mortals."

I took a deep breath and smiled as we entered the dining room to find Jack, Darla, Gunner and Jezebel enjoying beverages and a meat and cheese tray. I doubted Gunnar and Jezebel had brought the food, so I could only assume Mandy had provided the goodies. Nice touch, and one I'd consider for guests who arrived in the late afternoon to sate the pre-dinner munchies.

With a wave, a bald, heavyset man I didn't know grinned, then hurried over to introduce himself. "I'm Bruce, Mandy's husband. Welcome to our home."

"Thank you," I replied while imagining Adam quitting the sheriff's department and running my bed and breakfast with me. But could I put up with him full time? A loner by nature, I sometimes found it difficult to always have my ghost around. What about my boyfriend? Or would I one day be able to introduce him as my husband? Being involved with Darla's wedding definitely had me thinking about marriage more and more.

"Hey, Jezzy!" Ruby yelled. "Talking to you is like stepping on a leaf in autumn and hearing no crunch—a complete disappointment!"

Not one of her best, but I still couldn't repeat it to Jezebel since our hosts were in the room. The moment fell flat and even Jezebel's smile faded when our gazes met and she realized I couldn't deliver Ruby's zinger.

"Go ahead and have a seat," Mandy said. "What can I get you to drink?" Ruby pouted in the corner when she understood I wouldn't be forwarding her slight to Jezebel. Maybe the three of us could get together later and they could trade insults.

"Just some water would be wonderful," I said, sitting next to Gunner who took me into a big bear-hug, his thick black beard tickling my cheek and neck. With his huge physique, I sometimes wondered if he would accidently snap me in half when we embraced.

"We've heard all about the minister being murdered," he said. "This is awful."

I nodded as Mandy set down my glass. "Thank you," I said to her, then turned to Gunner. "How's Darla?"

"Needless to say, she's quite upset."

I glanced over at my friend who stared at the tabletop, seemingly off in her own world. What should have been a joyous time for her had turned awful.

"I think I'm going to lie down," she said, then stood and headed for the staircase.

When I rose to go after her, Jack shook his head. "Just let her rest."

Silence blanketed the room, along with a good shot of sadness. Poor Darla.

"What happened at the church?" Gunner asked, his focus on Adam.

As Adam explained he would be assisting in the investigation, everyone listened intently. He then repeated Ethel's story about Tricia.

"She sounds like a charmer," Jezebel said, rolling her eyes. "What an entitled little snot."

"We're definitely going to be interviewing her," Adam said. "She seems like a good place to start."

"If I can interrupt."

We all glanced over at Mandy. She and Richard had been so quiet I hadn't realized they were still in the room. "I hate George was killed, but there are other people who should be looked at besides Tricia Yeats."

"Who?" Adam asked. "Any help you can give us would be appreciated."

She smiled and laced her hands in front of her. "Well, there's been a lot of talk around town about the new minister who was brought in to help George with his duties."

"Why did George need help?" Gunner asked. "This is such a small town, I can't imagine the church being that busy."

"Yes, we're small, but look around. We live in one of the most beautiful places in the world. You all drove from Sedona to watch Darla and Jack get married. A lot of weddings are performed here. And, I'd also heard that George had recently been diagnosed with leukemia. He's slowed down quite a bit."

Adam furrowed his brow. "Why didn't Ethel mention any of this?"

"I don't know," Mandy replied, shrugging. "It's common knowledge in the gossip tree, and trust me, Ethel is one of the roots."

"Or the bee scattering the pollen," Richard

muttered. "I've never seen anyone spread more gossip than her."

It had been my exact impression upon meeting the woman, especially when Ethel mentioned she wasn't one to gossip. Red flag that indeed she was.

"Tell me about the new minister," Adam said, pulling out his notebook from his back pocket.

"Well, when George began to show signs of being ill, the mayor insisted he get checked out. Then, he was diagnosed. The weddings the church hosts don't only affect the bottom line there. It's the florist, my place, the motel, the restaurants... everywhere in town."

I fully understood. In Sedona, we all benefitted when there were events in town.

"We needed to keep the weddings going along with everything else like the weekly masses held, the funerals, the church events... but George wasn't up for it. So, the mayor brought in another minister."

"His name?"

"Paul." Mandy turned to her husband. "Honey, do you know his last name?"

"I don't. He's always just been Paul from the church."

"He's young, vibrant, and ready to change

things up around here," Mandy continued. "It's caused some friction."

"Although George was sick, he didn't look that elderly to me," I said, recalling Ethel had mentioned him to be around my age. "Forties are the new thirties, right?"

Mandy chuckled and crossed her arms over her chest. "Hey, I agree. I'm right there with you. But Paul is different. He's in his late twenties."

"And one hell of a good-looking guy," Richard said. "He belongs in a magazine selling expensive clothing and yachts, not preaching in our little church."

"Agreed," Mandy muttered as her cheeks turned the color of apples. "He's really something nice to look at."

"I can't wait to meet him," Ruby said. "He sounds like my kind of guy."

Based on the way Adam scribbled in his notebook, we would be crossing Paul's path sooner rather than later.

"What are all the changes he wants to make?" Adam asked.

"Well, for mass, he wanted to bring in a rock 'n' roll band that sings spiritual music to attract our younger population," Richard said. "But George likes the choir."

"Don't forget the pews," Mandy said. "Paul wanted to have them cushioned, saying more people would come to church if their rear ends weren't asleep from the hard, uncomfortable seats."

Recalling my stint on them, they most certainly could have done with that upgrade. My backside had gone numb with tingling pins and needles down my legs.

"He also wanted to replace the carpet and the stained glass," Mandy continued. "He said the stained glass wasn't environmentally friendly because it can get pretty drafty in there during the wintertime and in the summer, it's a little toasty. Basically, Paul wants to do a remodel on the place and bring it up to what he considered modern standards."

"George argued the windows and pews were part of the church's old-world charm and why did Paul want to change it into something that could be found everywhere?" Richard said. "Word is that it's led to some nasty fights."

But were the arguments bad enough to want to kill someone over it?

"Is there anything else we should know?" Adam asked.

Mandy and Richard exchanged glances and

shook their heads. "I guess I'm just surprised Ethel didn't mention any of that to you," Mandy said.

"Frankly, I am too," Adam muttered. "I'm not saying Paul did kill George, but we need to look into it."

"We've interrupted you enough," Mandy said. "Enjoy your afternoon and please let us know if you need anything."

No one spoke for a few moments after the couple filed out. As I reached for a slice of cheese and a cracker, I passed on my ghost's insult to Jezebel.

"That's weak," she said. "Ruby, you cause joy whenever you leave a room."

Everyone chuckled, lightening up the mood just a bit.

"Here's the deal," Jack said, staring in his glass as he swirled the remaining ice cubes at the bottom. "I want to marry Darla this weekend, and I want to get married in that church."

"It's closed," Adam reminded him. "We've got an open murder investigation. Remember?"

"I know that, and I'm really sorry George is dead. I want us all to work towards solving it in the next few days so my wedding plans can move forward."

Adam glanced around the table, as did I. We were a formidable crew. Adam had already been asked to help. Gunnar was also in law enforcement and could legally pitch in if his assistance was requested. Ruby and I had more than our fair share of experience in solving murders while Jezebel had mad fighting skills and got along with just about everyone. And Jack... well, he had a former life and special abilities I wasn't sure anyone knew about that may come in handy.

"What did you have in mind?" Adam asked.

Jack shrugged. "It sounds like we've got three people who need to be investigated: the bride, Tricia, Ethel the church lady, and now Paul, the new minister. Each has their own reasons for wanting George dead."

"How do you figure that?" Jezebel asked. "Especially Ethel. Why would she want her boss dead?"

"Who knows, but the fact of the matter is that she's a liar, at least by omission. Maybe she and Paul were working together to kill George."

"But why?" Jezebel pressed.

"We don't know," Jack replied, throwing his hands up in the air. "Maybe she wants the church updated as well and decided George was standing in the way."

"You've got a valid point," Adam said. "Ethel needs to be investigated."

"So does the bride, Tricia," I said. "She sounds like nothing but trouble."

"But to kill someone because they gave away your wedding date?" Gunner asked.

"Sure, why not?" Jezebel shrugged. "Maybe she became a psychotic bridezilla and mowed down the guy who had ruined her big day."

Everyone nodded in agreement.

"So, what's the plan?" Gunner asked. "How are we going to solve this murder so Darla and Jack can get married?"

CHAPTER 5

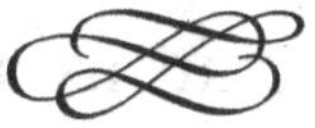

I LOVED that the bed and breakfast layout was similar to my own. Each suite had its own bathroom, which was good because I hated sharing. Even Adam's stuff annoyed me, but I put up with it because I loved him. The mattress had been wonderfully comfortable, as had the sheets. I'd actually pulled the bed apart after we woke the next morning so I could check out the mattress manufacturer and discover what the sheets were made of, because it certainly wasn't cotton. To my surprise, they were made from bamboo.

"We're going to have to pick some of these up," I said, typing the brand name into my phone. "They're pretty amazing."

"Agreed. I wasn't hot or cold," Adam said. He

gave me a quick kiss as his phone rang. "It's Sheriff Richards. I better take this."

As he spoke in low tones, I left the room to check on Darla, who was staying right across the hall. I knocked lightly, to no answer.

"I'll go in," Ruby said as she ghosted through the door. "Maybe I'll get to see Mr. Dimples in his skivvies!"

When she emerged, she shook her head. "Empty. No skivvies."

As Gunner's laughter and the smell of bacon filtered up the staircase, I realized everyone must've already gone downstairs for breakfast. I hurried down, eager to get the day started. But first, I needed coffee.

I found everyone in the dining room passing around heaping plates of eggs, bacon, and fruit.

"Bernie!" Darla said. "Good morning!"

The difference in her disposition both worried me and made me smile. She'd been so upset yesterday, I was glad to see her bright and cheery. Yet, I also became concerned when her mood swung to such extremes.

"Where's Adam?" Gunner asked.

"He'll be down shortly. The sheriff called."

"Are you ready for today?" He shoved a spoonful of eggs into his mouth.

"I am. I hope the plans don't change with the phone call."

"I'm sure she'll be fine with it," Gunner said. "She needs all hands on deck, and we've got more than enough motivation to solve the murder. She'll use us."

If she decided otherwise, I didn't know what to do with my time. I'd imagined us all enjoying the restaurants, the Riverwalk, and the shops. With Adam working, the idea didn't appeal to me as much.

A few minutes later, he came downstairs, his face grim as he dished up some breakfast.

"What did she say?" I asked.

"No civilians involved in the investigation," he replied. Of course, it made sense. Civilians shouldn't be trying to solve murders. "So you guys need to find something else to do today."

I glanced over at Jezebel, who arched an eyebrow. Darla's smile faded and Jack bit his lip as if to keep from saying what was truly on his mind.

"Where are you and I headed off to today?" Gunner asked.

"First stop is the sheriff's office. We'll go from there."

"What are you guys doing?" Gunner eyed the rest of us.

"We'll get it figured out," Jezebel said quickly. "You two better get going so you don't disappoint the sheriff."

"She's right," Gunner replied, sighing. "And here I thought we were going to have a nice vacation."

Jezebel kept her gaze focused on her plate but said nothing.

"We better get going," Adam said. "The sheriff said she wanted us there sooner rather than later."

The two men stood and we said our goodbyes. As soon as we heard the front door shut, Jezebel shook her head and pointed her fork at me. "We are *not* sitting around waiting for them to find the killer."

"Yeah!" Ruby yelled. "Let's go take down a murderer! Who cares what the sheriff says!"

"I'm really glad to hear you say that," Jack said, grinning. "I don't want to be sidelined, either."

"What do you say, Bernie?" Jezebel asked. "Are you in?"

Not only was I going against the sheriff's mandates, but what if Adam discovered we had our own side investigation? Maybe he'd appreciate the help, or he may become upset that we'd blatantly disrespected authority... again.

"Of course, she's in!" Ruby said. "She's not going to let anyone tell her what to do!"

She was right. I didn't like people telling me what to do. I preferred live and let live, but at the same time, there were lines that shouldn't be crossed—and I had a feeling I was toeing one of them.

"Let's be careful not to disrupt the investigation," I said. "But we can definitely feed them information."

"Do we know where Bridezilla lives?" Jack asked.

Mandy rounded the corner. "I can give you directions. I've lived here my whole life and know just about everyone."

She'd obviously been eavesdropping on our conversation. Helpful or creepy? We were in her house, and I was the first to admit that I also listened in on what my guests discussed. Yet, I don't think I ever made them aware of it.

"Very helpful. Thank you." Jezebel grinned and stood. "Then let's get a move on. We've got a murder to solve."

"CAN you believe how pretty this place is?" Jezebel asked as we drove down the main street of town. To our right stood the shops and restaurants, with the river and forest in the background. To our left, a wall of trees. Every now and then, we'd come upon a street sign on the left, which I assumed led up to the neighborhoods.

Turn left in five hundred feet.

I squinted up ahead trying to see the street but the thick foliage made it impossible.

"Dang. I would have driven right past this," Jezebel said, slowing down. "Thank goodness for Google Maps."

As we turned up Mayberry Street, we were once again engulfed in a thicket of trees. Every quarter of a mile or so, we'd see a cross street, but no houses.

Turn right in a half-mile.

The houses must have been nestled among the trees off Mayberry Street.

"It looks like we're being swallowed up into a horror movie," Ruby muttered. "The guy with the chainsaw and mask is going to step into the road at any second and cut you all to bits. It'll be a bloodbath. This is giving me the creeps."

I could see her point, but I didn't agree. Instead, I found it beautiful—nature at its rawest and strongest, barely touched by humans. Or at least, properly preserved.

"The phone shows the house should be up here on the left," Jack said.

Jezebel slowed and almost missed the dirt road. "I hate washing my car," she mumbled as she turned onto it and plumes of dust surrounded us.

A run-down two-story log cabin with a deck came into view, and it had definitely seen better days. Large trees swayed all around it in the afternoon breeze. On the side of the house, a tree with beautiful red flowers stood about ten-feet high, and I wondered what kind it was. Something like that would look wonderful in my yard.

Three cars sat out front, two without any wheels, the third a yellow Chevy carrying rust stains and a bumper held up with a bungee cord. Sacks of garbage had been piled by the garage.

"Okay, Darla and Jack, you stay here," Jezebel ordered. "You're going to be the backup in case Bridezilla gets physical. Of course, I'm sure I can handle her, but it's better to be safe than sorry." She pulled out her phone and Darla's began ringing. "Listen in to the conversation. If for any reason I feel we're in danger, I'm going to say lemons. Got it, Darla? Jack?"

"Yes," they replied in unison.

Jezebel shoved her device back in her pocket. "Bernie, hit record on your phone. Let's go."

She was expecting a physical altercation? If that was the case, I'd prefer to be on back up. Despite my months of self-defense classes with Jezebel, I still wasn't confident in my skills. Ruby, on the other hand, was thrilled I'd been chosen because she couldn't go more than fifteen feet away from me and enjoyed being in the middle of the action.

"Let's go kick some bride butt!" she yelled, shadowboxing in the driveway while I exited the vehicle.

As we approached the house, a woman stepped out on to the deck. She glared down at us and tossed her long blonde hair over her shoulder. "Can I help you?"

I had no idea what to say, but apparently Jezebel had given it some thought.

"Are you Tricia Yeats?" she asked.

"Who wants to know?"

Jezebel sighed and placed her hands on her hips. "I'll take that as a yes. We're here from the state office. We'd like to ask you a few questions about the minister at the church, George Tackle."

What?! State office?! State office of what exactly?

"What about him?"

"May we come up?" Jezebel asked, pointing at the rickety stairs.

"I guess so."

As the stairs groaned and moaned under our weight, I sent up a prayer they would hold us. When we arrived at the top, Tricia had taken a seat on a swing and she pointed to a table with two chairs. An old brown hound dog trotted out and sniffed my shoes as I sat down. After doing the same to Jezebel, he laid down at Tricia's feet and stared at Ruby.

"What are you looking at, handsome?" she asked. "Never seen a dead person?"

The dog wagged his tail.

"Who's the best boy in the world?" Ruby asked in baby talk. "Is that you? Are you the best boy in the world?"

As the dog's tail thumped on the deck, he rolled to his back and presented his belly. Ruby walked over, sat down and stroked him, continuing her baby talk.

"What about George?" Tricia asked.

"He's dead," Jezebel said. "Agent Maxwell and I are doing an investigation for the regulatory body that oversees the churches here in Arizona."

Agent Maxwell? Regulatory body? What happened to the division of church and state? Oh, my word. The lies were so thick, we may all drown.

Tricia nodded, seemingly oblivious to Jezebel's falsehoods.

"We understand there was some conflict between the two of you?"

"Yes. There was. But George had conflict with a lot of people in town."

"Can you tell us what happened between the two of you?" Jezebel asked. I gripped my phone in my pocket and hoped it was still recording. This was going much smoother than I could've imagined.

"He gave away my wedding date," she said, shrugging. "And I got really, really angry."

"Why did he do that?"

"Because he didn't agree with my choice of husband."

Wait a hot second. No-gossip Ethel had said Tricia hadn't paid her deposit.

"Why does he care who you want to marry?" Jezebel asked. "Who's your fiancé?"

"His name's Buck Ricker... Mayor Ricker's son."

"Why did the minister think your union was a bad idea?" I asked, now intrigued.

"He said Buck was a terrible influence. I mean, he's spent some time in prison and used to deal drugs, but people change."

Jezebel furrowed her brow. "When did he last get out of prison?"

"A month ago."

"Is he working?"

"Yes. For his father, doing the town landscaping."

"What did he say when the minister gave away your wedding date?" I asked.

She rolled her eyes. "He was livid. I mean, he's the *mayor's* son. We should get a little respect. But that's why George canceled the date—the old hag, Ethel, told me that. She said George worried for my soul if I married Buck and he wouldn't perform the marriage."

Jezebel and I traded glances. Quite the different story than the one we'd heard before.

"What did Buck have to say about that?" I asked.

"Oh, he was furious. Said he wanted to kill Minister George for dissing him like that."

"He said that verbatim?" I asked. Ruby had stretched out next to the dog and they lay face-to-face. His tail thumped against the deck while Ruby gently stroked him and whispered what a good boy he was, not paying attention to the murder investigation in the slightest bit.

"How did George die?" Tricia asked. "Heart attack?"

"No," Jezebel said, shaking her head. "It looks like he may have been murdered."

"Murdered!" Tricia screamed. "Oh my gosh!"

Very slowly, I could see her thoughts process. She'd just claimed her fiancé had threatened to kill the victim. "You know, B-Buck didn't mean what he said," she stammered. "He's had his troubles but he's a good man. I wouldn't get involved with a loser, and certainly not a murderer."

"We better get going," Jezebel said, standing abruptly. "Thanks for your time. We really appreciate it."

I followed Jezebel's lead and rose from my chair. Ruby sighed and stroked the old hound one last time.

"By the way," Jezebel said. "How long have you lived here?"

"My whole life. My parents died when I was young, so my grandparents raised me."

"Are they gone?" Jezebel asked.

"Yes. My grandmother died just a few months ago."

"I'm sorry for your loss," I said. "We appreciate your time."

"Wait!" Tricia said. "The one person you should look at for the murder is Doug. He's a homeless guy who lives by the river, usually staying under the bridge by the church. You can't miss him—long, greasy black hair. Really thin."

"Why should we talk to him?" Jezebel asked.

"Because when I was at the church, I saw him and Minister George yelling at each other. Apparently, Doug had robbed the church, and George was angry. Doug denied it and shoved George around a little bit."

"Interesting," Jezebel said. "Appreciate the tip. Thank you."

"Where did you two say you're from again?" Tricia asked.

"The state," I answered. "Thank you for your time."

We hurried down the stairs and once we were out of earshot, Jezebel whispered, "We've definitely got another suspect. That Buck is bad news. I believe he could've killed George."

"I fully agree. We need to track him down and

ask him some questions. I think we also need to pay Doug a visit."

"Yes. But let's keep our findings from Adam and Gunner for now until we get more information."

I hated hiding the truth from my boyfriend, but Jezebel was right. Until we found out who was lying, it was best to keep everything under wraps.

CHAPTER 6

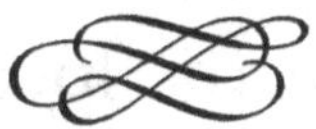

"SO, WHAT DO YOU THINK?" Jezebel asked as we drove back down to town.

"I think this town is filled with a lot of liars," Darla said. "Or maybe just one—the church lady."

"How was she when you booked your wedding?" I asked.

"Very nice and upbeat," Darla replied. "Very accommodating and she seemed excited for us, almost like a family member would be."

People were so complicated. Everyone had so many different masks they presented to different people. To me, Ethel had come across to be a hardened, weary woman. To Darla, she had offered up just the opposite. Who was the true Ethel? And did it matter? She'd been caught in a lie unless Tricia had made up the story of why her wedding was canceled. In any event, someone wasn't being truthful.

"Speaking of family members, Darla's mom is coming in today and should be here soon," Jack said. "She's staying at the local motel since we've taken up all the rooms at the bed and breakfast."

"We should get back to the B&B and get our car so we can meet her there," Darla said.

"Okay, we'll get you two dropped off and then Bernie and I are going to poke around a bit more," Jezebel said.

Great. I wasn't sure I wanted to do that, but I'd go along with her. Safety was best in pairs.

Mandy and Richard were pulling weeds in the front flower beds when we parked and I noted they had at least two dozen pansies of all colors ready to plant.

"Oh, those are pretty," Ruby gushed while Jack and Darla exited the car. "I love pansies."

As I stared at the yellow, purple, and pink little flowers, I remembered I also needed to freshen up my planters when I returned home.

"Okay, let's go," Jezebel said. "Bernie, come up to the front so I don't feel like a dang chauffeur."

I climbed over the seat and settled in.

"Now I feel left out," my ghost pouted.

"Ruby doesn't like sitting in back by herself," I said while buckling my seatbelt.

"Pretend you're the queen or something," Jezebel said. "She never rides up front unless she's at the wheel."

"Oh, I like that," Ruby murmured. "Drive me around like I'm royalty."

As we pulled away from the bed and breakfast, Jezebel asked, "Is she happy now?"

I nodded. "Jezebel, please return to the castle and fetch my crown. I seemed to have forgotten it," Ruby commanded in a high-pitched English accent.

"A royal pain in the butt," I muttered.

Ruby prattled on about her horse being prepared for her to ride when we returned to the castle and the Beef Wellington she wanted the chef to make for her.

"Who do you think we should go see first?" Jezebel kept her gaze on the road as she spoke.

After tuning out Ruby, I replied, "Well, we don't know where Buck lives and we know Doug resides down by the river, so I'd say Doug. Seems he'd be the easiest to find. I can't imagine a town this size has much of a homeless population."

"You're probably right about that," Jezebel said. "I don't think we should park at the church, though. If Adam and Gunner see the car, they may become suspicious of what we're doing."

"Agreed. Perhaps it's best to park on the other end of the Riverwalk and head up that way by foot."

"Good idea. Is the queen ready to do some sleuthing?"

I glanced over my shoulder. Her highness stretched out across the back seat and looked to be sleeping. Except, she was dead and had told me she never fully rested.

"Yes, I'm ready," she mumbled, sighing. "This vacation sucks."

She wasn't wrong. "Yes, we're ready to go," I said, turning to the front once again.

When we pulled in front of the gift shop and exited the car, the sun warmed my face and heat seeped through my Back to the Future t-shirt. I shut my eyes for a moment and enjoyed the sensation.

"Let's go," Jezebel said. "It looks like this path will lead down to the Riverwalk."

We followed the dirt trail, and the soothing sounds of the river rushing by became louder. When we emerged onto the Riverwalk, six Canadian geese stared at us from a small patch of grass.

"Don't go near them," Ruby warned. "Geese are nastier than a three-headed snake."

"And when was the last time you saw one of those?" I asked.

"Oh, be quiet. You know what I mean."

One goose stood to its full height and slowly approached us.

"Run for your lives!" Ruby yelled. "It wants to kill you!"

"Let's go," Jezebel said. "Dang, what a great day. We should be sitting on that deck right there drinking margaritas."

I glanced up at the Mexican restaurant and envied those who enjoyed the afternoon sun and cocktails.

"He's coming to eat your eyeballs!" Ruby yelled as she jumped in front of me. I glanced over my shoulder to find the goose trailing behind us, hissing.

"Get out of here!" I yelled, shooing him away. The dang bird didn't find me threatening in the least bit. Instead, I seemed to only make him more upset. Spreading his wings, he charged. I jumped out of the way, as did Jezebel. The goose hurried past us and began chasing Ruby. It had no interest in the living breathing women, only the dead one.

As I melted into peals of laughter, Ruby ran around me screaming, her arms up in the air.

"What's going on?" Jezebel asked.

She joined me in the laughter after I explained.

"Oh, I wish I could see that!" she said. "You deserve it, you old broad!"

We both laughed until tears rolled down our cheeks; people passing began to stare, and I imagined the scene looked absolutely silly to them—a goose appearing to chase nothing, honking as it ran in circles around two women giggling hysterically.

"This isn't funny," Ruby said as she hid behind me. "He's going to have to take you out first before he gets to me."

The goose charged again, going around me and heading directly for Ruby.

"Why does this thing want to kill me?" she screamed as she continued jogging around me.

"You're already dead," I said. "Maybe it hasn't seen a ghost before."

"Would you kindly leave so that I can get away from this thing?" she yelled.

I shook my head, knowing I would be punished later. The scenario was just too funny to end. "Sorry, Ruby. I haven't laughed this hard in a long time."

After a couple more minutes, the goose lost interest and waddled away.

"You're going to be so sorry for that." Ruby stood in front of me, her hands on her hips, scowling. "Mark my words, Bernadette Maxwell. Payback is going to be ugly."

"Is the commotion over?" Jezebel asked.

"Yes," I replied. "But I've got one upset ghost promising retaliation."

"That's not good," Jezebel said as we continued our walk. "Ruby was the best at revenge. Watch your back, Bernie."

"Yeah. Watch your back, Bernie," Ruby muttered. "Vengeance is going to be sweet. It may not come today or tomorrow, but it's coming for you. Mark my words."

Dang it. I'd be looking over my shoulder for weeks.

The rest of our walk—about a half mile— passed uneventfully. Ruby had gone silent, which worried me more than anything.

"I'm sorry," I said.

Ruby snickered. "No, you're not, but I'm going to make sure you are."

Ugh. I should've made more of an effort to save her from the goose. "But I am," I said.

"Stuff a sock in it, Bernie."

My word, she was upset.

"There's the church," Jezebel said, pointing up the hill. "And the bridge is straight ahead. Be on the lookout for a skinny guy with black, greasy hair."

As we approached the pathway under the bridge, I could see someone in the shadows sitting on a lawn chair against the wall, so as not to block the pathway.

"I think we've found our guy." Jezebel cracked her knuckles.

When he noticed us, he stood to his full height and walked out into the sun. Skinny. Greasy hair. "What do you two want?" the man said. "You can pass. I'm not going to bite."

"Are you Doug?" Jezebel asked.

"Why do you care?"

Jezebel sighed. "Okay, Doug. We just wanted to ask you a few questions."

His jeans hung loosely from his hips while his collarbones protruded from his too-big blue t-shirt. It was hard not to stare at the needle track marks in the crook of his arm. His right inner elbow had been poked so many times, it was black and blue with something oozing from the puncture wounds.

"That's nasty," Ruby whispered as she stared at it. "Why in the world would anyone want to do that to themselves?"

Excellent question.

"What do you want to know?" Doug asked.

"I understand you had a conflict with the minister from the church up the hill over there." She hitched her thumb over her shoulder. "I'd like you to tell me about it."

"No."

"Why not?" Ruby asked. "What are you hiding, buddy boy?"

"It's none of your business." Doug pursed his lips. "It's *my* business."

Jezebel and I exchanged glances. "Can I tell you what I heard?" I asked.

He shrugged. "If you want to."

"You and the minister got into an altercation because he believed you stole from the church. Did you?"

He stared at me a long moment. "I took some things, but I was going to bring them back. I didn't mean to cause trouble. I just wanted to make George mad."

"What did you take?"

"Some papers from the office. They always leave the doors open and I waited until Ethel and George were gone. I wanted to inconvenience them."

"Why?" Jezebel asked.

"Because George is always telling me that I need to turn my life around and change. I'm happy the way I am. I like living here." He glanced behind him at the bridge. "I keep to myself and leave everyone alone. I don't hurt anyone and I want him to mind his own business."

"Well, I don't think that will be an issue any longer," Ruby muttered. "George will definitely be leaving you alone."

"Did you know George is dead?" Jezebel asked.

Doug didn't confirm or deny. He simply stared at her for a long moment, slowly spun around, and returned under the bridge. As he lowered himself to a seated position and leaned against the wall, a woman jogger entered the tunnel from the other end.

"Hey, Doug," she said, breathing hard.

"Hi, Sam."

As she passed us, I realized it was the woman who had sold me the bath bombs at the farmer's market. She wore her salt and pepper curly hair in a ponytail, her thin frame covered in black leggings and a sweatshirt. She certainly held no fear of the man living under the bridge.

Perhaps Doug was simply a community fixture, not a dangerous killer.

"We've got to figure out who that woman is," Ruby said. "We know her, I'm just not sure from where."

"I don't think we're going to get anything more out of him," Jezebel said.

"Me neither."

"Same here," Ruby chimed in. "I think the conversation is over."

As we turned to head back to the car, disappointment settled in my chest. I had hopes that the man under the bridge would confess and it would be the end of the investigation. He'd seemed like a perfect candidate for a murderer... until I met him. Yes, he obviously had some drug issues, but that didn't equate to being a killer.

"Hey!" Doug called. The three of us stopped and glanced back at him. "George got what he deserved! Just remember that!"

CHAPTER 7

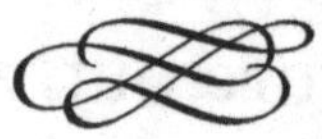

DESPITE US QUESTIONING DOUG FURTHER, he had nothing to add. In fact, he simply told us not to steal anything from his pile of belongings and walked away.

That evening, as we recounted the day to Gunner and Adam, they both listened intently. Neither were upset we had gone against the sheriff's directive.

"She's out of her element on this one," Adam recounted. "She's never run a murder investigation... never had to living here in Heywood. We need all the help we can get."

"Do we know who Doug is?" Gunner asked. "Like a last name, how he arrived in Heywood, where he came from? Any history?"

"No," I replied. "He seems like a town fixture, though. A woman jogged by him while he was sitting under the bridge and said hello. She wasn't afraid of him in the least bit."

"And we still need to figure out who the heck she is," Ruby said. "Don't forget that's on the to-do list."

Yes, I was curious because I thought I recognized her, but a murder was just slightly more important than discovering her identity.

"Interesting," Adam said. "What's Doug's story? Do we know who the woman is? Can we question her?"

"Yes," I replied. "I bought some bath bombs from her at the Farmer's Market. I have her store name on the product and receipt upstairs."

"She may be someone to speak to if she was comfortable with Doug," Adam said. "Hopefully, she can provide some background on the guy. What was your perception of him?"

I furrowed my brow and pursed my lips to hide my smile while I remembered the goose chasing Ruby. I'd share that with Adam later when I was sure no one could hear me speaking about my ghost. Mandy and Richard were nowhere to be seen, but that didn't mean they weren't lurking around a corner eavesdropping.

Well, at least that's what I did in my bed and breakfast. I had to assume the same for them.

"Earth to Bernie!" Adam said.

"Sorry. I got sidetracked. What did I think of Doug? I actually felt sorry for him. He seemed harmless. Troubled, but not a danger to anyone."

Gunner shook his head. "Drugs make people do horrible things," he said. "Doug could've killed the minister and not even remember doing it."

"A total blackout," Jezebel said in agreement.

My knowledge of heroin addiction was limited at best, most of it coming from television shows where people shot up and then passed out.

"If there's heroin, there's most likely other illegal substances being abused as well," Gunner explained. "Probably some booze mixed in, too."

Jezebel stood. "Speaking of which, I'm going to track down some beers."

"What did you two do today, Adam?" I asked as she headed for the kitchen.

He reached over, grabbed my hand, and gave me his best grin that always made my heart skip a beat. "Nothing as exciting as you. We went through the papers in the church office."

Gunner rolled his eyes in the back of his head and let out a long snore. "It was beyond boring. Give me a run in with a drug addict any day."

"Ugh," Ruby said. "Agreed, Gunner. Papers should be used to start fires."

Jezebel returned and set down four beer bottles, already popped open with wisps of condensation rising from the mouths. My instincts must have been correct: our hosts were listening in and trying to stay one step ahead of our needs. There was no way Jezebel could've retrieved the bottles and opened them so quickly.

"It wasn't that bad," Adam said, chuckling. "Come on. Wedding invoices? Funeral plans? The employee records of the after-school care staff? What could be more gripping and thrilling?"

"Oh, yeah, that's a snooze fest if I ever heard of one," Jezebel said. Gunner laid his head on her shoulder and she tapped his cheek. "My poor boy isn't cut out for mundane work like that."

As a former undercover cop, Gunner's career had been dangerous at best. After his last job, he'd gone into regular police work with Adam, which pleased Jezebel immensely. Worrying about him had been in the forefront of her mind for too many years.

"Did you find any paperwork regarding Tricia's wedding?" I asked. Hopefully there'd be some notes that explained why she'd lost the date:

Was it the deposit or George disliking the man she'd chosen to marry?

Adam took a long swig of his beer, then glanced at Gunner with a furrowed brow. "I don't recall anything. Do you?"

"Nope. Maybe when they gave the date to Darla and Jack, they shredded it."

"Perhaps, but there was stuff in there from a decade ago," Adam said. "I don't know a lot about the workings of church, but it seems like they kept every shred of paper."

"True," Gunner replied. "Including contracts from canceled events."

"How strange," I murmured. "Can you look for it again tomorrow?"

"Sure, but why?"

As I recounted our visit to Tricia's house and her story varying so much from Ethel's, Gunner and Adam listened intently. "So, in a nutshell, she said the minister didn't like that she was marrying Buck and this was why the wedding was canceled."

"But she also had it in her mind that the church should've given her more leniency with the deposit," Jezebel said. "Buck's the mayor's son."

"I'm confused," Adam said. "Because she's

marrying the mayor's son, she didn't think she'd have to pay the deposit on time?"

"Yes," Jezebel and I said in unison.

"And why didn't the minister want her marrying him?" Gunner asked.

"Buck has had some legal issues," Jezebel said. "The kid's bad news. Drugs and prison time. According to the minister, he's a bad influence on Tricia and he didn't approve of their pending nuptials."

"Is that any of George's business?" Gunner asked. "Did he really get a say on who gets married at the church in this town and who doesn't?"

"Apparently," I replied, shrugging. "If what Tricia said is true. Her version of events is miles away from Ethel's. Remember? Ethel said they didn't pay the deposit. Tricia claims Minister George canceled the wedding on moral grounds."

"We need to talk to Ethel again," Gunner grumbled. "Someone's lying."

"Tricia did say that Buck was angry about the wedding and he told her he wanted to kill the minister for canceling the date," Jezebel said.

Adam arched an eyebrow then traded glances with Gunner. "How in the world did you get her to admit that?"

"She didn't know the minister had been murdered at that point," Jezebel replied. "After she threw her fiancé under the bus, she quickly pointed us toward Doug."

"Do you guys think Tricia and Buck could've murdered George over their wedding date?" Adam asked.

"People have killed for less," Gunner said.

"Do we know what killed George yet?" I asked.

Adam shook his head, then took a long pull of his beer. "He was definitely poisoned. We need to wait back for toxicology to find out with what."

"Does the sheriff still think it was in the coffee cup?" Jezebel asked.

"Yes."

"We need to talk to the people at that coffee shop," Gunner muttered. "What was it called?"

"Cup of Go," I replied, recalling the name with ease because I'd thought it was so clever.

"Cute name," Jezebel said.

"We need more people to help us," Gunner said. "What about Sheriff Walker? Did you get a hold of him, Adam?"

He nodded. "He'll be up either tomorrow or the next day."

"Oh, wonderful!" Ruby squealed. "I get to see Bruce-y Boy!"

She'd been so quiet, I'd almost forgotten she was around. But of course she was. She couldn't go more than fifteen feet away from me when outside our house.

"We can definitely put him to use," Gunner said.

"Agreed," Adam replied. "We need to talk to a lot of people because the suspect list keeps growing."

~

THE NEXT MORNING, Darla and Jack went with her mother to see the sites, which also included a boat tour of the lake downstream. Adam and Gunner took off to do police-y things, and Jezebel and I decided to head to Cup of Go with Ruby in tow.

"Bernie, this is your version of heaven right here," Ruby said. "Books, coffee and pastries."

She wasn't wrong. I immediately fell in love with the store.

On the far-left wall stood floor-to-ceiling bookcases filled with novels, self-help books, history tomes... just about anything one could want to peruse. A long counter filled part of the space and we stepped in line to order. Tables and chairs had been placed strategically around the store, making it feel larger than it was. Artistic lighting hung from the high ceilings, and of course, the windows on the far side offered a breathtaking view of the river. About a dozen customers drank coffee and either chatted, were hunkered down in front of a computer, or intently reading a book.

As I glanced over the bookshelves, I wished we had time for me to grab one along with a cup of coffee and make myself comfortable for a few hours.

"Hi," I said to the barista when our turn came. "Vanilla latte please."

"Make that two," Jezebel said.

"Coming right up!" Our server, whose nametag read Sierra, grinned and hurried to make our orders, her blonde bob bopping around her shoulders.

"How do you want to bring up the minister?" I asked while we waited.

Jezebel shrugged. "I figure direct is the best approach."

Once we were served and had paid, Jezebel slid a twenty-dollar bill across the counter and smiled. "Can we ask you a couple questions about the church minister who used to come in here all the time?"

"I guess so," she said, stuffing the money into her pocket.

So much for the direct approach. Jezebel went straight for bribery.

"Was he a regular?" Jezebel asked.

"Yes. Every day. I don't recall a time when I was working that he didn't come in. George was his name. Most days, he came in once in the morning and then again in the afternoon."

"And he was a nice guy?" I asked.

"Most definitely. He'll be missed around here. I heard he died."

Apparently, word hadn't gotten out he'd been murdered.

"Did anyone ever stop in and say they were picking up a coffee for George?" I asked.

Sierra shook her head. "Not that I recall."

"Were you working Tuesday afternoon?" I asked.

As she pursed her lips and stared at the ceiling, I almost glanced up to see if her schedule was written there. "I worked in the morning and got off about two."

"Is there someone here who was working that afternoon shift we can talk to?" I asked.

She turned to her co-workers. "Were you guys working on Tuesday afternoon?"

One young guy raised his hand and approached warily. As he ran his hand through his thick, long brown hair, he reminded me of those men from the old romance novels, except he couldn't be a day over seventeen. Or, perhaps he was in his twenties. The older I became, the younger everyone else appeared to be. "What's up?" he asked.

"We were wondering if you saw the minister, George, come in here on Tuesday afternoon," I said.

The kid shook his head. "George didn't, but Minister Paul did. He's the new dude over at the church."

Jezebel and I exchanged glances, and my heart began to race. "And do you remember what he ordered?"

"Sure do," our new friend replied, his voice strong and sure of himself. "He bought two coffees—one for him and one for Minster George. He even knew his usual."

"And what's that?" Jezebel asked.

"Decaf with sugar free hazelnut syrup and a sprinkle of cinnamon."

"What's the point in drinking that?" Ruby asked. No caffeine? No sugar? No one's life should be that tasteless and boring."

"So, Paul came in here and ordered two coffees, one for George," I said. "Did he say anything that struck you as strange?"

He shook his head. "Not really. He said he was trying to mend fences with George by bringing him a coffee."

"Did he happen to mention why he needed to make peace with George?" I asked.

"Nope. Just asked us what George's usual was and said he was hoping they wouldn't fight anymore."

Well, they wouldn't fight again if he spiked it with poison.

"Was he acting nervous or strange?" Jezebel asked.

"Nah. It's Minister Paul. He's a cool guy."

"Thanks," I said as someone behind me cleared their throat. We'd held up the line long enough.

Jezebel and I took our coffees and stepped outside while Ruby hummed and danced next to us. Once again, irritation ran through me. I would love to spend some time at the coffee shop, sitting by the windows, enjoying a book and the view, but this dang murder was taking up all our vacation time.

"What do you think?" Jezebel asked. "Paul

came in the day George was poisoned and ordered his favorite coffee. The sheriff thinks the coffee is what killed him."

I took a sip of my latte. Yum. Hopefully it wasn't poisoned, but it tasted good enough that I'd chance it. "I think we should go report back to Adam and Gunner. We may have just found our killer."

CHAPTER 8

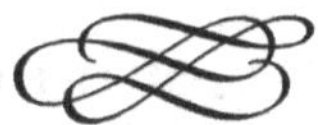

ADAM AND GUNNER mentioned they'd be at the church again today, so Jezebel and I took the Riverwalk up to the church, sipping our coffee. Another beautiful day in Heywood.

"I have to admit, Bernie," she said, "I'm getting a little irritated with this whole situation."

"What do you mean?"

"I came here expecting a vacation, to spend some time with Gunner and enjoy the town. I mean, look at this place." She stuck out her arm and spun around in a slow circle. "It's awesome." She pointed at a group of river rafters laughing as they floated by. "I want to do that. I want to know the history of this place, to eat at every restaurant, to go on tours, spend time in all the shops... and instead, I'm looking for a killer."

With a sigh, I nodded. "I feel the same way, but we're doing it for Darla. We may not see the sites, but we can try to find the murderer, open the church, and watch her get married this weekend."

Jezebel took a sip of her coffee. "I suppose you're right. Here's to Darla." We tapped cups and continued our walk.

"Maybe we can arrange to visit at some point in the future," I said, having very little hope of that happening. Getting time off together had been difficult for Adam and Gunner, and Sheriff Walker had only allowed it because they were attending a wedding. Jezebel had left her bar, Tip 'Em Back, in the hands of one of her employees. My business had closed completely as I had no one to run it. We'd all made great sacrifices to be here for Darla and Jack's wedding. Personally, I couldn't close my doors on a whim. I needed to keep the money rolling in. Some months, I barely scraped by, while others, I had a windfall of cash. Staying in business was a delicate balancing act.

"Perhaps," Jezebel muttered. With her tone of defeat, I could only guess her thoughts mirrored mine.

As we climbed the path to the church and

walked around to the front door, I noted an empty parking lot. Gunner and Adam weren't there. Just as we were about to turn around and head back to the Riverwalk, a blue Toyota pulled up. The man exiting was nothing short of a perfect specimen of the human male species.

"Holy cow," Jezebel whispered as we stood and stared.

In his twenties, tall, lean, with a headful of black hair and the most perfect jawline I'd ever seen, he pulled a bag out of the backseat, then caught us staring. With a bright smile, he waved and I swear I swooned. But I wasn't quite sure because I'd never swooned before.

"Take a gander at that hottie," Ruby said. She laced her hands on her head and swiveled her hips. "Come to Mama, lover boy. I'll show you how it's done."

"Oh, for Pete's sake, knock it off," I hissed. "You're so gross."

My ghost threw her head back and cackled while Jezebel asked, "What's she doing?"

"Being vulgar and inappropriate."

"Ah, my favorite side of Ruby." Jezebel chuckled. "My guess is that fine man right there is the famous Minister Paul."

"Agreed," I whispered as he marched toward the front door like he owned the place.

"Excuse me!" Jezebel said, jogging over to him. "Can we talk to you for a second?"

"Sure," he replied, grinning again. How in the world did he get his teeth to be so white? "What can I do for you?"

"Are you Paul?" she asked as I approached.

"Yes."

"I wanted to talk about George's death," Jezebel said.

"Yes. A terrible tragedy. Are you with the police?"

"Sort of," she replied. "We are directly tied to the investigation."

"I see. What can I do for you?" When he met my gaze, his ocean-colored eyes glittered with... happiness? Mischief? I wasn't sure. Whatever it was, it looked good on him.

Interesting how he didn't question how we were involved in the investigation. Was he a pretty man, but stupid? Or did he just not care?

"How long have you been at this church?" Jezebel asked.

"I was brought in about six months ago, give or take a week or two," he said.

"To help George?" I asked.

"Yes. He had some health issues."

"Where were you before?"

"California," he replied, and I cringed. As a general rule, Arizonans welcomed people to the state, but they didn't like the politics that often came with west coast transplants. A trend of, "Don't California my Arizona" had begun and picked up steam every day.

Jezebel crossed her arms over her chest. "Were you happy to be assigned here?"

"Most definitely," he said, stretching his arms wide. "Take a look around! Who wouldn't want to live here?"

"Yes, it's gorgeous," I said, sighing and wishing we were having fun and enjoying the sites instead of hunting a killer.

"We understand there were some issues between you and George," Jezebel said.

He shrugged and pursed his lips. "That's no secret. Yes, we had our differences."

"Would you care to elaborate?" I asked.

Paul glanced over his shoulder at the church, then turned his attention back to us. "Well, I see the potential in this place. George... George didn't want to move into the future. Instead, he wanted to keep things just the way they are."

"What changes did you want to make?"

Even though I'd heard Mandy's version, I listened intently to the minister for his.

"This church could become the epicenter for worship in this area," he said, his eyes gleaming with excitement. "To do that, we need people to come, to tithe and spread the word. Once we build up the coffers, we can expand and become a mega-church for Northern Arizona."

"And how do you achieve step one?" I asked. "Getting people into your church?"

He smiled and a flush washed over my skin. Goodness, he was handsome. *And remember, you have a dang boyfriend!*

"Well, first, we need new blood. We need to re-energize the church. Choirs are the old way, and let's face it... they're as boring as watching paint dry. Young people don't want a choir. They want something they can relate to. There are so many Christian rock bands looking for a place to play, we could have a different one come in every week."

"What else?" Jezebel asked, staring at the old stone church.

"Get rid of the stained glass," he said, waving his hands in the air. "Put some new cushioned pews in so people are comfortable. Update the inside to make it more exciting, more modern, and once the building is overflowing, we raze this to the ground and build a larger, more modern church!"

I glanced at the ancient building that looked as if it had been around since the beginning of time. Yes, it was old, but it fit in with the community. Personally, I liked it just the way it was. I tried to imagine a larger, contemporary structure standing in its place.

"With my plan, we could serve our community and the surrounding areas so much better," Paul said.

"This guy is all about ego," Ruby muttered. "He wants to be one of those mega-church ministers that rake in millions of dollars a year from their flock."

"But the guy in charge didn't want to move in that direction," Jezebel said.

He nodded and sighed, the disappointment that he'd met opposition to his plan evident. "And neither did Ethel. Like I said, we need new blood."

"So are you the guy in charge now?" Jezebel asked. "The top dog?"

"Yes, yes, I am," he said, grinning. "Once I let Ethel go, I'm going to put my plans in place. First and foremost, upgrade the office so it's all digital, then get someone in there who's good with computers and social media. That's step one."

"Why doesn't he show any remorse about George's death?" Ruby asked, tapping her chin with her pointer finger. "It's almost like he's happy his fellow man of God bit the big one."

"Tell me about the day George was murdered," Jezebel said. "I understand you bought him a coffee?"

For the first time, his smile faded. "No, I didn't."

Wait. *What*?!

"You didn't bring George a coffee on the afternoon he died?" I asked, hoping for clarification.

"No, I didn't."

Jezebel and I traded glances while her brow furrowed in confusion.

"Okay," I said. "I thought we'd heard that you stopped into Cup of Go and ordered George a coffee. You two were fighting and it was a peace offering, or something like that."

He shook his head and pursed his lips. "No, sorry. I'm not sure who would give you such misleading information, but that never happened."

Completely stunned by his falsehoods, I was left speechless. Or was he telling the truth and the kid at the coffee shop lied?

On the other hand, Jezebel seemed to be able to form sentences. "Do you know why Tricia Yeats' wedding was canceled?" she asked.

Paul shook his head. "You'd have to ask Ethel about that. I stay out of the day-to-day planning. She takes care of it with George's guidance. Well, *took* care of it."

"He can't wait to get rid of her," Ruby said. "Ethel's a goner."

And he was going to have to start dealing with the mundane day-to-day tasks if he was going to build his mega-church.

When tires crunched on the pavement, we all turned. A police cruiser.

Sheriff Mallory Richards stepped out of the vehicle. "Uh oh. You're going to get thrown in the slammer!" Ruby exclaimed.

I took a deep breath, grasping for feasible lies in case she questioned us about being at the church. Having been specifically told not to interfere with the investigation, we were going to be in trouble if Paul mentioned what we were discussing.

Mallory's gaze narrowed as she approached us. "Aren't you two Gunner and Adam's girl-friends?"

"Yes, they are," Ruby said. "Arrest them!"

I nodded and smiled, hoping to appear friendly.

"What are you doing here?" she asked.

"They were questioning me about George's death," Paul said. "Wondering about my plans for the church."

The sheriff arched an eyebrow. "Oh, really? I thought I asked Adam and Gunner to keep civilians out of the investigation. Didn't you two get the memo?"

"We did," Jezebel said. "We were just chatting with the minister. There's no law against that, is there?"

A brief second of doubt flickered in Mal's eyes, then she shook her head. "No problem talking to the minister, but I would appreciate it if you two would stay away from the church and everyone involved in it."

"I'll be heading inside, then," Paul said with a smile.

"Sorry, it's closed for another day or two," Mallory said. "Can't let you in."

His smiled faded. "That's too bad. I have a few things in there I'd like to pick up."

"Well, you'll have to wait." Her voice indicated there would be no further negotiation.

"We're going to head back to the bed and breakfast," I said. "Nice to meet you, Paul."

As Jezebel and I went down the pathway back to the Riverwalk, I felt the sheriff's stare on us.

"What the heck was that?" she whispered. "Who's lying? The kid at the coffee shop who said Paul brought George the coffee, or Paul?"

"Why would the kid at Cup of Go lie? He doesn't have a stake in any of this."

"True," Jezebel said. "We should go back and see him to make sure he's talking about Tuesday afternoon. Maybe he's thinking of a different date?"

"Don't bother," Ruby chimed in as she spun around in circles next to me.

I turned to her. "Why not?"

"Because the handsome holy one did it."

"Well, it looks like he lied, but what else has happened that makes you think he's the killer? The kid at the coffee shop could've been mistaken."

Ruby rolled her eyes. "Oh, jeez. Use your brains, girl. Mr. Hot Stuff back there obviously wants big things for himself. A huge church and an enormous flock to listen to him. All that comes with a thick wallet, as well. With George out of the way, he can fire Ethel, and no one is standing in his pathway of glory and fame on his way to Heaven."

"What's she saying?" Jezebel asked.

As I explained Ruby's theory, Jezebel nodded. "She's right. He's got motive and means."

We stared at each other a beat, and I scrunched my nose. "Do you think we were just chatting with the killer?"

"Trust me," Ruby said. "You most definitely were."

CHAPTER 9

WHEN ADAM and Gunner arrived back at the bed and breakfast, I was already curled up in under the sheets with a book, feeling sorry for myself. Like Jezebel, I'd been looking forward to having fun on this trip. Instead, I was completely alone while the sheriff stole Adam's time away from me. I'd tried calling, but his phone went directly to voicemail. I sighed in frustration when the doorknob turned.

"Hey," he said, walking in and shutting the door.

"It's really late, Adam," I replied. Glancing at the clock, it read almost eleven. "I've been trying to call."

He stretched out next to me and sighed. "I'm

sorry. My phone went dead and I didn't have a charger. I stayed at the church late to try to track down the paperwork on Tricia's wedding."

"Did you find it?"

"No. I have notes regarding events that may take place. They have paperwork from over a decade ago. But nothing on that wedding."

"Perhaps it was misplaced," I said.

"Or maybe someone doesn't want it found for some reason we can't understand and it's been destroyed. It seems weird to me that it's missing."

"We saw the sheriff today," I ventured, wondering if she'd mentioned our run in.

"She told me. You were speaking with Minister Paul, correct?"

"Yes. Jezebel and I were actually looking for you and Gunner at the church. When we got there, Paul pulled up, so we decided to have a little chat with him."

Adam turned to me. "Learn anything new?"

"I'm not sure yet," I said, appreciating he didn't seem angry with me for butting into the investigation. "We talked to a kid at Cup of Go who said Paul brought George a coffee that afternoon. Paul denies it."

"That's interesting. What did the kid look like?"

"Longish hair that he tossed around like he was Fabio."

Adam sat up and furrowed his brow. "I stopped in to Cup of Go this afternoon. Paul was there talking to a kid matching that description."

"Did you hear what they said?"

He shook his head. "I remember Paul seemed really upset. I thought maybe the kid had gotten his order wrong. They were talking quietly, but based on his scowl, it was obvious Paul was angry."

"I wonder what that was about?" I asked.

"Our Greek god minister was clearly telling the kid to keep his mouth shut," Ruby chimed in. "I bet if you go ask the Fabio wannabe again, he'll have nothing to say about Paul."

Ruby could very well be right, and I intended to confront the barista. Well, someone should. Someone with a little authority would most likely be best.

Adam shrugged. "I'm not sure, but I'll have the sheriff question the kid to find out."

"Why not you? Or Gunner?"

"Because we've got other plans tomorrow," Adam said, grinning. "Special plans."

As he took my hand in his, a little jolt of excitement rushed through me. "What does that mean?"

"We're going river rafting. It's going to be a blast."

"Seriously? Oh, my gosh! I've been watching them float down the river and it looks like so much fun!"

"Yeah, Gunner and I got everything set up to-day. Jack and Darla are going with us as well."

"Where do we start? What time?"

"Our launch time is eleven and the staging area is upriver a ways. We'll float by all the shops and end on the other side of town. Then, they take us back to our cars."

"Oh, that's going to be a good time," Ruby squealed. "I can't wait!"

I wasn't sure how river rafting would work with my ghost. Would she sit on the raft next to me? Hover above me? Sink? I supposed I'd find out, and I wouldn't worry about it. After all, she was dead, so nothing horrible could happen to her.

"Does that mean we can spend the rest of our time in Heywood having fun?" I asked, trying not to get my hopes up. "Or are you still helping with the investigation?"

"No, I'm still helping out," he said. "But we

have a bit of a reprieve for a few hours tomorrow."

I smiled through my disappointment.

"We better get some rest," he said.

As he brushed his teeth and turned out the lights, I stared at the ceiling, too excited to sleep. At least for a few hours, I'd be able to forget about the murder, the wedding, and the investigation.

We'd have a small window of actual vacation time, and I planned to enjoy every minute of it.

THE NEXT MORNING, I was up at the crack of dawn. Adam snored lightly beside me while Ruby sat in a chair watching us sleep.

"Oh! Thank goodness you're up," she said, jumping to her feet. "I thought I may die of boredom. Let's go do something! Aren't you excited about rafting? How about we go buy a bottle of tequila to take on the trip? Trust me, rafting is always much more fun with tequila."

After shooting my ghost a glare, I got dressed and exited the room. As I crept down the stairs, I realized I was the only person up and about... well, except for my ghost who was still rambling on about tequila.

I decided to drive into town and hit up Cup of Go for a pre-rafting trip vanilla latte. Since they'd just opened, I was one of the first in line. The barista, Fabio, as I'd nicknamed him, was standing behind the counter, and I smiled as I approached.

"Good morning," I said, glancing at the pastries.

"'Morning."

After placing my order, I grinned again. "Do you remember our conversation about the day Minister George died?"

"Yep."

"I just wanted to confirm that Paul came in and got him a coffee that afternoon."

He wrapped up my muffin and shook his head. "I was wrong. It was the day before."

Narrowing my gaze, I searched for signs he was lying, but found none.

"Seriously," he said. "I was wrong."

Or had Paul been threatening him when Adam had seen them talking?

Deciding not to push the issue, I paid and grabbed my steaming cup of goodness, then searched for a chair. All the tables by the windows overlooking the river were taken. I selected a mystery novel from the bookcase, then chose a seat by the front door. Disappointment flooded through me that I didn't have a view of the river.

I read for a few minutes, then glanced up at the street outside. Slowly, the town came alive. Shops opened, restaurant staff arrived, the garbage truck did its rounds, and in the distance, the sound of a chainsaw caught my attention.

Who would be using a chainsaw this early in the morning? I shut my book, more interested in the happenings in front of me than the words on the page.

As I sipped my coffee, the sound drew nearer. More people filed into Cup of Go, looking for their caffeine fix.

"Do you think that's the town slasher?" Ruby asked, cranking her head to see down the street. "He's starting off the morning with a bloodbath?"

I shrugged, a little curious myself. No one ran by me screaming for their life, so I had to assume whoever was behind the whirring machine was harmless.

As I debated another latte, the person wielding the chainsaw came into view—a worker trimming the hedges lining the street. He stood about six feet with military trimmed black hair and broad in the shoulders, wearing a short-sleeved shirt that read, *City of Heywood Land-*

scaping. As he ran the blades over the foliage, they dropped to the cement, and I noted another man a few yards back sweeping up the droppings into a trashcan on wheels.

I studied the tattoos on the chainsaw-wielding man's forearms. *Tricia* had been inked on in script lettering. When he turned toward Cup of Go and wiped his brow, his name tag said Buck.

Bingo. The groom.

"Hey!" Ruby yelled. "That's Buck!"

"Way ahead of you on this one," I muttered.

Forgetting my second latte, I hurried out of the store and tapped him on the shoulder. With a jolt of surprise, he glanced at me then flipped the chainsaw to the off position. I smiled, hoping I appeared friendly.

"You shouldn't sneak up on people like that," he chastised me. "I could've hurt myself or you. I'm assuming you like your appendages right where they are. I know I do."

"I'm sorry about that," I said. "I was wondering if I could speak to you for a minute."

"What do you want?"

Pointing to his inked arm, I said, "Well, I spoke to Tricia the other day, and I was hoping I could take a few minutes of your time."

He narrowed his gaze on me. "She told me

someone was poking around in our business. Who are you?"

"I'm with the state," I said, hoping he believed the lie as easily as his fiancée had.

"What does that even mean?" he asked, rolling his eyes. "What state? A state in the United States? There're fifty of them, in case you weren't aware."

"I-it means I'm here in an official capacity," I stuttered. This wasn't going how I'd planned. Apparently, I didn't convey the same authority as Jezebel. Or he was simply smarter than Tricia, which, from what I'd seen, wouldn't be too difficult to achieve.

He shook his head and chuckled. "I'm not buying your story, but you've got me curious. What do you want to know?"

"You're the mayor's son, correct?"

He nodded. "Yeah. You'd think old Daddy would give me a better job, right?"

"When did you get out of prison?" I asked, ignoring his question. From what I'd heard about his past, he was lucky to have old Daddy give him a job and a second chance.

"A month ago, but you already asked Tricia about that."

Correct. I wanted to be sure we didn't start the conversation off with him lying.

"Can you tell me what you were in for?"

"Fighting. Drugs. The usual stuff."

"Lots of murderers behind bars, too," Ruby interjected.

"Why do you think Minister George canceled your wedding?" I asked.

After setting down the chainsaw on the pavement, he rolled his shoulder and massaged it. "He doesn't like me. Doesn't like my family, even though my dad's in charge of the dump."

"That doesn't seem very godly," Ruby muttered, and I had to agree. I had a hard time swallowing the fact George didn't like who Tricia was marrying, so he quashed the wedding. It really wasn't his place to do so. The lack of deposit leading to a canceled wedding made more sense to me.

"Tricia said that you mentioned you wanted to kill George." I wasn't asking a question—I just put it out there and searched for a reaction.

"Yeah, I did. I mean, I'm the *mayor's* son. I *deserve* respect. My dad is the most important person in town. He should've been *begging* me to get married in his stupid, dumpy church."

Buck's entitlement surprised me. Not that being a mayor of a small town was anything to sneeze at, but he seemed to want to be treated like royalty. "Did you consider following up with killing George?"

He snickered and shook his head. "Yeah, I did. I even went to the church one night and keyed his car. I also stole some stuff. But I never laid a hand on him."

I wasn't sure I believed him, but decided not to question him any further about it. Time to change tactics. "So, when are you and Tricia tying the knot?"

"Don't know," he replied, shrugging. "I know it won't be here in town."

"Why is that?"

"George was an okay guy. Sure, he really made me mad, but in the end, you could tell he cared. Paul… Paul's a self-centered jerk."

"Says the entitled little snot," Ruby scoffed. *Duly noted.*

"Why do you say that?" I asked, wondering if the sentiment was common around town.

"He's got big plans for the church. Wants it to become the mega church for Northern Arizona. Between you and me, I think he just wants to line his pockets and mattress with a bunch of bills. He doesn't care about this community. Even my dad has regrets about bringing him in to help George."

Paul did have a lot to gain with George's death—no doubt about it.

"I appreciate your time," I said. "And I hope you and Tricia find a nice place to tie the knot soon. You two seem perfect for each other."

"Yeah, both young, dumb, and full of themselves," Ruby said. "Absolutely perfect."

I waved as I headed toward my car. George had angered Buck about the wedding. Buck had said some threatening things he shouldn't have. But did that mean he'd killed the minister?

"Hey!" Buck called.

After I turned around, he said, "And quit asking questions about me. You won't like what happens if you continue."

With that threat, Buck moved up a couple of notches on my list of likely murder suspects.

CHAPTER 10

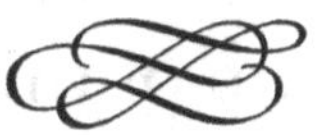

Later that afternoon, we drove up to the staging site and I lathered on my sunscreen.

"The sun is good for you," Ruby said as I rubbed another layer into my arm. "Vitamin D. Things like that."

"It also causes wrinkles and skin cancer," I muttered, applying more to my nose. "There's nothing wrong with me taking precautions."

"No, there's not, but you've got enough of that stuff on for three people. It's really a little overkill, Bernie. It's not even disappearing anymore. You look like someone rubbed zinc oxide all over you. Ridiculous."

"Can I get some of that?" Darla asked from the front seat. "I don't want to burn."

"This is what's wrong with your generation," Ruby grumbled, shaking her head. "You're afraid of everything, even the sun."

Before we could argue, Jack turned the SUV onto a dirt road. "We're here," he announced. "It should be at the bottom of this hill."

We slowly rolled down the unpaved path and a parking area came into view.

"Woohoo!" Ruby squealed as we pulled into a space. "I can't wait for this!"

The drive had taken about a half hour, and it felt great to stretch my legs when I exited the car.

Gunner and Jezebel parked next to us, and the six of us—well, seven, counting Ruby—made our way down to the shore, laughing and joking with each other. We were greeted by a shirtless, tanned man in his twenties with blond hair and a friendly smile. "I'm Jordan," he said, introducing himself. "I'll be your guide today."

"Well, hello there, Aquaman," Ruby purred. "Do you need me to towel you off?"

As I shut my eyes and shook my head in frustration, I was once again so thankful that no one but me could hear her.

After a safety lecture when we were told to always do as Jordan said or we could end up in the water, we donned our lifejackets. The sun's reflection off the river was so fierce, I wondered if I had enough sunscreen on. I wished I could wear my hat, but they were forbidden as they could be lost in the river. "We don't want to be responsible for your headwear's demise," Jordan joked. "Besides, we don't need your ugly hats ruining our beautiful river!"

I couldn't imagine losing my hat while peacefully floating down the river, but I was a rule follower, so I hiked up to the car to place mine in the backseat, then returned to the launch pad.

"Oh, my goodness," Ruby said. "I'm so excited! I'm going to sit next to Aquaman!"

We all piled into one large, circular orange raft. Thankfully, Adam held on to me. When I slipped on a rock, I almost ended up flat on my back and bruised from the rocky shore.

"Watch yourself, there, Grace," he said, chuckling.

Although Ruby wanted to sit next to Jordan, there wasn't room for her to sit anywhere, so she issued a string of curses and hovered near me.

Once we were settled in, Jordan showed us where to hold on and reminded us to do exactly as he instructed. "We don't want anyone to end up eaten by alligators!"

"There's nothing funny about that," I griped,

making sure there weren't any gators floating around. It wasn't the right environment for them... was it?

"Sure there is," Ruby said, laughing along with him. "Lighten up, Bernie. Besides, there aren't any alligators. I think I saw piranhas were indigenous to this area."

Shut up.

Ruby cackled and shook her head. "Oh, your face... you want to tell me to stick it where the sun don't shine. Relax. Nothing will happen. How many people have we watched float by without being attacked by gators or piranhas, just enjoying their day?"

Quite a few. River rafting seemed to be one of the main attractions while visiting Heywood.

"Let's do this!" Gunner yelled, clapping his hands.

"Right on, man!" Jordan shouted and they high-fived.

"Boy talk is so cute," Ruby mused.

Jordan pushed us out into deeper water and then hopped on the raft in one graceful, agile move. As he used a paddle to maneuver us out into the middle of the river, to my utter horror, Ruby crawled into his lap. I noted the goosebumps traveling over his skin as her presence sent a cool gust of air over him. "Wow! Do you guys feel that cool pocket?" he asked.

Adam and I traded glances, and I shook my head. I wasn't going to explain Ruby's antics. Maybe later.

Ignoring my grandmother's impropriety, I glanced around at the scenery. Tall green pines sandwiched us on both sides. Birds sang in their branches. A breeze whispered against my face, and I smiled. What a perfect day.

To my surprise, Jordan gave us a little history of the town as we gently floated. "Founded in 1876, Heywood was a mining town, as well as a logging town. They used the river to float the wood downstream to the lake."

"Oh, be quiet," Ruby muttered. "Let us enjoy this without you prattling on like some talking parrot."

Jezebel, however, had other ideas, and she asked a lot of questions. Like Ruby, I sort of wanted silence. I tipped my head back, closed my eyes, and tuned out the conversation to concentrate on the water lapping against the raft.

"Bernie, check this out!" Ruby yelled.

I opened my eyes and found her standing on the side of the raft between Jezebel and Darla. She stepped back and disappeared, but then reappeared a few seconds later. I rolled my eyes, not impressed. In the past, I'd seen her jump off cliffs, which had scared me. Her antics now were weak in comparison, but I couldn't say anything and interrupt Jordan's history lesson.

"Oh, wait!" Jordan said in a hushed tone, turning to us. "Look to the left! There are two deer on the bank!"

The graceful, gentle animals stared at us with their big brown eyes as we floated by.

"So pretty," Adam whispered, and I nodded in agreement.

Once we'd passed the deer, Jordan raised his voice again. "Okay, we've got some rapids coming up, so remember what I said earlier: *Hold on and do what I tell you!*"

Wait a minute. Rapids?! I hadn't signed up for rapids! I realized there was a significant portion of the river I hadn't seen lying between the launching site and Heywood town center. My idea of a lazy day float quickly vanished as I heard the rushing water up ahead.

"Oh, my gosh," I whispered.

Adam laid his palm on my shoulder. "It's going to be okay," he said, smiling reassuringly. "We signed up for this!"

"I didn't," I countered, slapping his hand away. "And do what Jordan says—hang on."

"Here we go!" Jordan yelled. Our raft bounced on the first rapid, sending a wave of cool water into my face. With a gasp, I quickly wiped my eyes and grabbed my handle again.

Jordan maneuvered us through the rocks, each rapid seeming rougher than the one before. All my friends whooped and hollered, having the time of their lives. How had I not known we'd be tossed around like rag dolls and soaking wet? I glanced around for Ruby but didn't see her. Had I lost my ghost?

More water sprayed up at me as I heard Ruby's laugh from above me. I tore my gaze from the river ahead and found her floating above me. "This is funny to watch," she called, giggling. "You look terrified."

She wasn't wrong. If I had only been more prepared and knew what to expect, perhaps I'd enjoy this wet rollercoaster a little more.

"Relax, Bernie!" she yelled. "Jordan's done this a lot of times. He's not going to let anything happen to you! And maybe next time you should listen to your old grandmother and get the tequila when I tell you to!"

The bouncing and water to the face continued

a few more minutes. A couple of times, my butt actually left the raft and I gripped the handle so hard, I feared I'd snap it off. My friends whooped and hollered, having a fantastic time. Apparently, I was the only one unaware this would be a wild ride. The others were enjoying themselves way too much, while fear gripped my chest. If only I'd been prepared…

Finally, the river calmed. I sputtered and tried to pull the wet strands of hair from my cheeks and eyes. The rest of my crew laughed and shouted. When Adam pulled me close, I realized I still had a death grip on my handle. Slowly, I un-clenched my fingers.

"Your fingers are white," he said, smiling.

"I guess I was holding on for dear life."

"You weren't expecting rapids?" he asked.

I shook my head. "No. It never even occurred to me. I thought we'd be floating calmly down the river for a couple of hours."

Thwap.

What was that sound? Probably just the water lapping against the raft. I settled into Adam's em-brace as we went under the bridge and asked Jor-dan, "Will there be any more rough water?"

"Nope! It's smooth sailing from here on out."

"Dang it! I wanted some more," Jack said.

"Me, too!" Darla agreed. "That was amazing!"

"Come by tomorrow and we'll go on the expert route," Jordan said. "If you want some real excitement, that's the way to go."

The ride hadn't been thrilling enough for my friends? I'd definitely be skipping the expert level.

Thwap.

We'd reached the part of the tour that I'd expected the whole time. Calm waters. Beautiful scenery. Relaxation.

Except, why was water filling up the bottom of the raft? Sure, we'd hit some pretty big waves, but water seemed to be seeping in despite the calm waters. Glancing over the side, I heard another *thwap,* and I realized the problem.

Someone had shot arrows into the raft and we were now taking on water.

CHAPTER 11

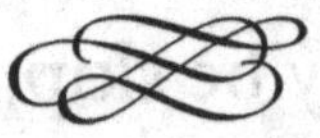

"Oh, heck," I whispered as I stared at the offending object that would put us under water in no time. "Jordan!"

He glanced at me, his face contorted in confusion when he noticed the water rising at the bottom of the raft. He'd been so focused on the river ahead, he hadn't seen the issue.

"What's going on?" he asked.

"There's… someone's shot arrows into the raft!"

"Holy cow!" Ruby yelled. "We're going down, just like the Titanic!"

"Okay, everyone stay calm," Jordan said as he surveyed the area. "Here's the deal. We've all got lifejackets on, but we're in a really deep part of the river. We won't be able to stand, which means we'll have to float downstream."

As he pulled a radio wrapped in plastic from his vest and mumbled into it, I studied my friends. Darla's wide eyes indicated panic. The rest of them simply seemed uncertain, waiting quietly for directions from our leader.

I stared at the hole, the tip of the red arrow barely visible. The water continued to flow in. Panic gripped my chest, but I reminded myself I could swim. But what I couldn't do was tackle anymore rapids on my own.

"Listen up," Jordan said as he paddled to the right. "I'm going to try to get us over to the river's edge. If we don't make it there before we sink, they're ready to catch us downstream. Usually, this wouldn't be that big of a deal and we could simply stand up down river, but the waters are really heavy this year because of the record snowfall we had."

"How do they catch us?" Darla asked.

"They're placing a rope across the river, from shore to shore, and some of my co-workers are going to be there to help grab us.

"What happens if we somehow make it past the rope?" Jezebel asked.

"There are some really intense rapids on the

other side," Jordan said. "If you don't stop yourself at the staging area, you better start praying."

Oh, heck. That's exactly what I didn't want to hear.

Between the currents and our weight, Jordan did his best to get us to shore, but it seemed like a futile effort, even when we all started paddling along with him. I now sat with water up to my knees and I realized I'd have to take my chances on someone catching me downstream if I couldn't make it to land.

Another minute of frantic paddling went by, and I glanced up, seeing that we now floated by the center of town. People sat out on the decks of restaurants sipping their drinks and eating their food, completely unaware of our predicament. A couple of fishermen gave us strange looks as we coasted by, but what could they have done?

One of them called, "Do you need help?"

"I think we'll be okay!" Jordan yelled. "We're going down, though!"

"Let's stick together, Bernie," Adam said. "No matter what happens, you stay close to me, okay?"

I nodded, somewhat shellshocked by the experience. In the meantime, Ruby was screaming something about me not being selfish like Rose and not allowing Jack on the doorframe. I assumed she was referring to the movie, Titanic.

As I sat waist deep in water, I realized we weren't going to make it to shore.

"We're going to have to float down river!" Jordan shouted. "We've taken on too much water!"

Adam grabbed my arm and pulled me away from the raft. As I struggled to find my footing, I remembered we were in a deep area of the river. Anxiety froze me for a second as the currents carried us downstream.

I had issues trusting other people. That was why I never hired a cleaning person to help me with the bed and breakfast—I had trouble believing they'd do a good job. Yes, I relied on Darla to provide my guests with amazing breakfasts, but she was my friend and we had trust built up between us. Now, my fate was in the hands of people somewhere up ahead I'd never even met.

"Grab onto this loop," Adam ordered, placing my hand onto the side of his life vest. I found the strap and gripped it tightly.

Behind me, I heard Jezebel yell, "Let go of it!"

Adam and I glanced back to find Gunner straining to hold on to the raft, his face twisted with effort.

"Drop it, Gunner!" Adam called. "We'll see if we can get it later!"

Why the heck did they want a dead raft?

"We'll need it!" he screamed and grunted.

I couldn't imagine the weight he fought. The raft had completely submerged and he wrestled to drag it with him. No matter how strong a man was, how much weight he lifted, he was powerless against Mother Nature.

Gunner made one last attempt to bring it with him downstream while Jezebel cursed at him. "It's going to take you under, you idiot! I'm not going to lose you because of a stupid raft! Drop it!"

After giving it one more try, he let go and swam toward Jezebel and she slapped him on the head, a gesture followed by a quick kiss.

Where in the world were Darla and Jack?

Somehow, they'd made it to shore. They stared at us wide-eyed as we rounded the bend, and I worried I'd never see my friends again. With the way this trip was going, it was a distinct possibility.

Jordan swam ahead of us, the currents working with him and carrying him swiftly.

"We should be coming up on the rope pretty soon," Adam said. "Don't let go of me, Bernie, okay?"

"You said that already."

"Yes, but it's important. I'm holding on to you, but I don't want us to get separated."

As I nodded, I once again tried to catch my footing. Still nothing. At some point, the river would become shallow again, right?

"Remember to breathe!" Ruby shouted from above me. "Your anxiety has you all knotted up and you aren't breathing!"

Of course, she was correct, but I couldn't take any deep breaths with water splashing in my face every few seconds.

Up ahead, four men dressed in orange vests came into view. They bobbed in the river about five feet apart from each other, and I realized they held on to a rope that had been strung across from bank to bank. This was it. I either grabbed one of them or the rope, or I risked my life on some intense rapids down river.

As Adam and I raced toward them, Jordan arrived before us and grabbed the rope, then turned toward us. They shouted at each other and pointed, then moved to place themselves in front of us. Three of the rescuers hurried towards the area where Jezebel and Gunner would meet the rope, while two placed themselves in front of Adam and me. I figured Gunner needed three to stop him and Jezebel simply because of his huge size. Jezebel wasn't any waif, either.

"Grab onto the rope! Grab onto the rope!" they shouted as we approached.

I kept my eye on the men in front of me as they bobbed in the water, each holding on to the line.

"Make sure you grab onto them or you'll decapitate yourself on that rope," Ruby warned. "That's something that would happen to you."

"Not helpful, Ruby," I muttered. "Not helpful at all."

I held onto Adam's life jacket and reached forward as we approached.

"Here we go!" the man in front of me yelled.

Mother Nature delivered me directly into his chest. "Take the line!" he screamed in my ear as he wrapped a thick arm around my waist. Glancing over to Adam, I wanted to be certain he had reached safety before I released his life jacket. He held the rope and also had one of the men gripping his life vest at the collar.

With both hands, I grabbed the line, the man still holding onto me. "Let's get to shore," he said. "Slow and steady. I've got you and you aren't going anywhere."

As I placed one hand in front of the other and

slowly made my way toward the riverside, the currents fought to take me downstream. I'd never been so happy to get to land when I felt it beneath my feet. Once I could stand, making my way to the riverbank became infinitely easier. When I was fully out of the water, I pulled off my life jacket and collapse on the rocks. Adam sat down next to me, breathing heavily.

Gunner and Jezebel quickly followed. Jordan offered us each a bottle of water and a towel while one of the other men asked us if we had any injuries.

All four of us shook our heads as the rest of them removed their life vests.

"What about Darla and Jack?" I asked. "They made it to shore in town."

"We've already sent someone to fetch them," one of the older men said. Maybe in his fifties? Possibly sixties? "I'm Harold, and I'm the owner. What happened?"

"Someone intentionally took out the raft," Adam said, his voice now clipped and official, or what I called "cop mode."

"Intentionally?" Harold asked.

"Yes. Someone was shooting arrows at it."

"And they had good aim, too," Ruby said. "They didn't even hit anyone, only the raft."

"Arrows!" Harold exclaimed. "Who in the world would do that?"

I didn't know if someone had been shooting at the raft hoping to drown us and did have good aim, as Ruby had suggested, or the arrows had been meant for our bodies, and had missed their target. But who would want to hurt or kill us, and why?

"We better call the police," Harold announced. "I'll grab my phone."

My phone. After reaching for mine and worrying I'd either find a waterlogged device or I'd lost it at the bottom of the river, I realized I'd left it in our car up at the raft staging area. Relief flooded through me as I sipped my water.

"I'm really pissed," Gunner muttered. "That was calculated. What if one of us had been hit?"

"And who would want to do that?" Jezebel asked. "Do you think it was meant for us, or was it directed at the rafting company?"

That hadn't occurred to me. Maybe we had nothing to do with it and we were simply the unlucky passengers.

"Let's think this through," Adam said, pushing his wet, blond locks off his forehead. "Who would want to either scare or kill us?"

"The murderer we're trying to find," Gunner growled.

"Where were we when you first noticed the arrow in the raft?" Adam asked, turning to me.

"It was right after the bridge," I said. "Doug, the homeless guy, lives there."

"We're going to pay him a visit right now," Adam said, standing.

"I'm going to beat his face in if he did this," Gunner said.

"Oh! A fistfight!" Ruby squealed as she shadowboxed. "I love a good rumble!"

"No, you aren't," Jezebel chastised. "You're an officer of the law and you'll act like one. That doesn't include beating in anyone's face."

We all staggered to our feet as Harold returned to us.

"Does your rafting company have any competition in town?" Adam asked. "Anyone who'd want your business to suffer?"

"Sure, there is," Harold said. "But I can't imagine he'd go to these lengths to put me out of business."

"You never know," Gunner said. "Either those arrows were meant for us, or they were meant to damage your reputation."

With a furrowed brow, Harold shook his

head. "I'll talk with Tony, but man, that's some messed up stuff if he did this."

"Can you please take us back to our car right now?" Adam asked.

"The police are on the way," Harold replied, shaking his head. "They'll need statements."

"We're working with Sheriff Richards," Gunner said. "We'll check in with her later. Right now, we have some things to do."

Just then, a jeep pulled up and Darla and Jack exited. "Oh, my gosh!" she said, running toward us. "I was so scared!"

We assured her everything was okay, after which Harold ordered Jordan to return us to our cars.

As we piled into the Jeep, exhaustion settled in. I could barely keep my eyes open as we slowly drove through town, stopping every few feet for pedestrians. Stress sometimes had that effect on me. I either became wound up, or I completely shut down after nerve-wracking situations.

"Stop the car!" Gunner ordered.

I glanced out the window. The church lay just ahead, so that meant the bridge was right around here. Gunner had said he wanted to ask Doug a few questions and apparently, he wasn't going to wait.

Before Jordan could pull over to the side of the road, Gunner had exited the vehicle with Adam on his heels. Jezebel, Darla, Jack, and I trotted behind them.

When we arrived at the bridge, Doug was nowhere to be found.

"Dang it!" Gunner shouted, his voice echoing off the bricks.

Although I was now shivering in my wet shorts and t-shirt, I walked over to Doug's pile of belongings. I found the missing paperwork from the church, including the notes on Buck and Tricia's wedding, which wasn't a surprise since Doug admitted he'd taken paperwork from the church office. But there on top of the papers lay a red arrow, just like the one I'd seen buried in the side of the raft.

CHAPTER 12

AFTER SEARCHING for the bow without any luck, we returned to the bed and breakfast for hot showers, Adam carrying the arrow to take into the police station for evidence. As soon as they were in dry clothes, he and Gunner left for the sheriff's office.

Jezebel, Jack, and Darla decided wine was in order and headed to the back porch. Not in the mood for afternoon cocktails, I ventured out with Ruby.

"Where are we going?" she asked as I slid into my SUV.

"I thought we'd go see that woman at the herbal store," I replied. "She seemed to know

Doug, and since no one can track him down, I figured she could shed some light on him."

"Like if he's a psychopath who likes to play cowboy and Indians with real arrows?"

"Yes. Exactly."

As we drove through town, I studied all the buildings, searching for the herbal store, Sage Advice. I found them tucked away next to Knit Wit, a knitting store.

"Cute name," Ruby said.

I nodded as we exited the car. "Don't touch anything," I hissed before opening the door. "Promise me."

"Fine, fine," she said, crossing her fingers.

"Say it. And finger crossies don't negate your promise."

She rolled her eyes and sighed. "I won't touch anything."

"Thank you." The scent of fresh plants, mint, and lavender accosted me as we opened the door. On the far-right wall stood a floor-to-ceiling bookcase filled with books and labeled jars. Thyme. Kava Root. Ashwagandha. Milk Thistle. I had no idea what the benefits were to using any of them. At least Ruby wouldn't be detected while we were in the store. She smelled too similar to the offerings.

"Hi, there," the woman behind the counter said, grinning. Once again, she seemed familiar to me with her salt and pepper long, curly hair and pretty face. I wish I could remember where, when, and how we'd crossed paths.

"Hi," I said. "I was wondering if you have a few minutes to talk with me?"

Her smile faded slightly, but she nodded. "Sure. What's up?"

Maneuvering my way through the display tables, I longed to stop and study everything: soaps, tinctures, bath bombs, teas... it all smelled amazing and I wanted to read about their benefits.

"My name's Bernie, by the way," I said, leaving off the spiel of me being here with the state. She obviously wasn't stupid enough to believe it.

"Sam," she replied as we shook hands. "It's nice to meet you. Did I see you at the Farmers' Market on Tuesday?"

"You did! I bought some bath bombs."

"That's right. I thought I recognized you. Have you had a chance to try them out?"

"Unfortunately, no." I'd been too busy trying to find a killer and avoid being a victim. "I saw you jogging the other day by the river. You said hello to the man who lives there. Doug. I was wondering if you could tell me a bit about him?"

Her shoulders slumped. "Here I thought you were going to have some serious questions for me. What do you want to ask me about him?"

"How long have you known him?"

She tapped her pen on the counter. "I've been here about a year. I guess my first encounter with him was right after I arrived."

"What was that?"

"I was jogging along the Riverwalk and my wallet fell out of my pocket just as I passed his set up under the bridge. He chased me down to give it back to me. Scared me to death at first because I didn't know why the homeless man under the bridge was screaming at me and running after me. Finally, I took out my earphones and realized he was trying to return my wallet."

"Did… did he take any of the money out of it?"

"To my utter shock, no," she said, shaking her head. "I had ten dollars in there when I left my house and I had ten dollars when I arrived home."

Returning the wallet and not taking any money? That certainly didn't sound like someone who would purposely shoot arrows at a raft.

"The second time I met Doug, I stopped while jogging and introduced myself," she continued.

"He was a little out of it then. I think he'd just done some drugs, but he was still polite. I offered to buy him a sandwich for returning my wallet to me, but he declined."

"You aren't afraid of him," I said.

"I'm originally from Los Angeles. Homeless people with drug problems are a way of life there. One guy under a bridge doesn't scare me."

"From Los Angeles to Heywood is a pretty big culture shock," Ruby said. "I wonder what happened to have her make that leap?"

I did as well, but it wasn't any of my business.

"Don't take this question the wrong way, but why do you think they allow Doug to live under the bridge?" I asked. "This place is pretty pristine."

"How would I take that the wrong way?" the woman asked, grinning. "I agree. We have this amazing little slice of heaven that caters to tourists. A guy living under the bridge on one of the most beautiful walkways is a strange thing, and the town allows it."

"Why?"

"Because he's related to Mayor Ricker. A cousin or brother... something like that. I'm not really sure."

"That's the second person who's close to

George's death who's related to the mayor," Ruby said. "Buck is his son, and now Doug is also kin. That's really interesting."

I wasn't sure how it all fit together, though. "So the mayor gives him permission to live under the bridge?" I asked. "Why doesn't he take him off the streets? Give him a place to live?"

"That I don't know," Sam replied. "Families and their innerworkings can be pretty messy."

Something flashed in her eyes. Pain? Knowledge of the messy family?

"What can you tell me about Buck?" I asked.

"Not much, only the gossip I've heard."

"What's that?" In a town this size, I knew the chin-wagging tree had to be pretty large, its roots stretching far and wide.

Sam glanced at the door behind me, probably to be certain no one would come in and catch her spilling the tea.

"I really don't like to gossip," she said. "It's toxic and it can hurt people."

"She knows from experience," Ruby said. "This woman's been through the social wringer at some point."

"I'm from out of town," I said. "I won't reveal where I got my information."

"Why do you want to know about him?" she asked.

Deciding to go with the truth, I said, "My boyfriend and I came to Heywood to watch our friends get married. We were planning on using the trip as a vacation, to spend some time together. We're from Sedona where I run a bed and breakfast and he's in law enforcement. We don't have a lot of free time. Now, with the minister murdered and the sheriff department being overrun with the flu, the sheriff has asked for my boyfriend's help to solve Minister George's murder. We haven't gotten that relaxing vacation. I'm just trying to gather information so that I can pass it on to Adam. Maybe, just maybe, we can have a free day or two and watch our friends get married."

"What an awful trip," Sam said. "That's a real shame."

"It is. Buck was angry at George. I'm trying to fill in a little background detail on him."

"Have you spoken to him?"

"Yes, I have. He's not a nice person."

"No, he's not," she said, grinning. "I've had a couple of dealings with him myself. It's never been pleasant."

"Why is he like that?" I asked.

She sighed and shook her head. "I think it comes down to entitlement. He's had a very, very easy life and he screwed it up by getting involved in drugs and fighting. From what I hear around town, people were hoping his stint in prison would calm him down, but it didn't. When he came back here, no one would give him a job, so his father put him on landscaping duty. As my grandmother would say, the man has a black heart."

"What do you mean by an easy life?" I asked.

"Well, his family is very wealthy. Not like celebrity wealthy, but they don't have any money worries and their table has never been bare. Nice vacations, summer camps, fast cars, boats... you know what I mean?"

I nodded.

"Buck was a good kid until he graduated high school. It all went downhill from there with the fighting, the drinking, and the drugs. My understanding is that he did a semester at Arizona State University, but then got expelled."

"That's a shame. He really messed his life up, going from college to prison."

"All in the span of two years," Sam agreed.

"Do you know anything about his fiancée, Tricia?"

"I've only seen her around town. I've never spoken to her."

"What can you tell me about her?"

Sam shrugged. "There's a lot of gossip regarding their impending nuptials."

"What do they say?"

"Basically, she's a small-town girl with big dreams and she thinks marrying into Buck's family can get her what she wants."

"Do you think they had anything to do with George's murder?" I asked.

"I have no idea. Why would they?"

I explained that Ethel had claimed the ceremony had been canceled due to the lack of deposit while both Buck and Tricia had said it had been because George didn't like Buck.

"Huh. I wonder which one is the truth?" Sam mused.

"I don't know," I replied. "I feel like I'm running around in circles trying to figure this out."

"Maybe you should leave it to the police," she said, winking.

"You're probably right, but like I said, I'd rather find the killer and at least have a couple of days of vacation. If I can give them information to make that happen, then I'll be one happy woman."

"I hope you get to enjoy everything Heywood has to offer," Sam said. "We do have some weird and quirky people here, but I can't imagine anyone murdering George."

"Well, someone did."

"You know, word on the street is that Buck is trying really hard to get his life back together," Sam said. "I heard he's been saving up to open a river rafting company."

"Oh, really?"

"Yes. I was told he's saving every last nickel he can. Even entering in some shooting competitions and pocketing the winnings."

"Shooting competitions?"

"Yes. Both him and his father are expert marksmen for both guns and bow and arrows."

"Holy cow!" Ruby yelled while I stared at Sam, stunned.

"Are you okay?" she asked. "You look a little pale."

"I-I'm fine," I whispered. She hadn't heard about the rafting incident earlier in the day. I gave it twenty-four hours before the story made its way into the store.

I'd assumed the arrows had been aimed at us, but Jezebel had suggested they may have been meant for the rafting company. If Buck wanted to open one for himself, perhaps he was trying to put the competition out of business?

But then again, he'd threatened me when I talked to him earlier in the day. Now that I knew he was an expert marksman, I wondered if they had been meant for me. But I would think an expert marksman would've hit me? Or was he just trying to frighten me?

And if that was the case, Buck looked better and better for the murder. If he was going to go to such lengths to either hurt his potential business competition or scare a woman vacationing in his town, he could definitely kill a guy who had canceled his wedding, regardless of the reason.

CHAPTER 13

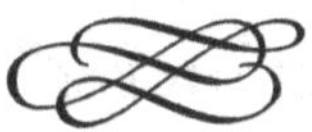

WHEN I ARRIVED BACK at the bed and breakfast, I found everyone gathered in the backyard. The sun had begun to set, the sky colored with beautiful hues of pink, purple, and blue visible through the tall pine trees. Jezebel, Jack, and Darla had polished off two bottles of wine. With their glassy eyes, pink cheeks, and lazy smiles, they seemed to be enjoying themselves, and I wished I'd stayed and helped them.

"You just missed my mom," Darla said. "She headed back to the hotel."

Glancing at the two empties, I asked, "Did she drive?"

"Oh, no," Darla said. "Mandy took her back for us. Wasn't that nice?"

"It was." I was relieved no one had attempted to operate a vehicle. Some of the roads leading into town were a bit windy and it wouldn't take much to end up in the ditch, especially with wine running through one's veins.

"Did you just get here?" I asked Adam as I took a seat at the wooden picnic table and poured myself a glass. I wasn't going anywhere else except to bed.

"We did," Adam replied, sipping his beer. "Where have you been?"

"Talking to the woman at Sage Advice," I replied.

"Why did you go there?" Gunner asked.

"Because she knows Doug. I wanted to get some background information on him."

"What did she have to say?" Darla asked.

I explained Doug was related to the mayor and pretty much harmless. "I don't believe he was the one who shot at the raft. But Buck... he may be a different story."

"Why is that?" Gunner asked.

"Because he's an expert marksman with a bow and arrow, as well as guns, and also has plans to open a rafting company in the near future."

Adam furrowed his brow. "You think he's trying to take out the competition?"

"I don't know. He also threatened me, so I'm still not sure if the arrows were for me or the rafting company."

"When did he threaten you?" Adam said, balling his hands into fists. "Maybe I need to have a chat with him."

"I saw him this morning when I went for coffee. Everyone was asleep. It was a weak threat, and one I'm certainly not worried about."

"Why didn't you tell me?" Adam asked.

I shrugged and sipped my wine. "Because it wasn't worth mentioning."

"Your boyfriend's about to go all macho man," Ruby said. "No one messes with macho man's woman."

I smiled while Adam took a big gulp of his beer. Ruby was right. Poor Buck would be mincemeat if Adam wasn't a cop.

"That doesn't sit well with me," he muttered.

"It's not a big deal, Adam," I said, deciding turn the conversation away from Buck. I didn't think he was dangerous—all bark and no bite, despite his love of fighting. "For the record, I doubt Doug killed anyone, either."

"You have no proof," Gunner said. "He had a fight with George. He could've killed him while on drugs."

"Sorry, I have to disagree, especially if we believe George was poisoned. People out of their minds on drugs don't plot a murder like that. I would think if he'd been responsible, it would be more of a spur of the moment thing. Besides, how did he get the poison into the coffee?"

"She's got a point," Adam muttered. "Maybe it's time to cross Doug off the suspect list."

Gunner shook his head and finished off the rest of his beer. "No way, man. He's staying on mine. That guy's squirrely as heck."

"You think everyone's squirrely," Jezebel said.

"Very true," Gunner said, standing and stretching his arms over his head. "This day has worn me out. Are you coming up to bed, Jezzy?"

She nodded and also stood. "I drank too much wine."

Darla and Jack quickly followed behind them, leaving Adam and me alone. Well, and Ruby.

"Was it something I said?" I asked, gesturing toward the empty seats.

He chuckled and shook his head. "Between the rafting debacle and the wine, I think everyone was done with the day."

Frankly, I was too, but I didn't have the energy to head upstairs quite yet. "What did you do this afternoon?"

"We went with the sheriff to the church for a bit, then back to the station where we met George's ex-wife."

"Why was she there?" I asked.

"Because Mallory wanted to interview her."

A slow grin spread over Adam's face.

"What happened?" I asked. "I can tell your chat with her was interesting."

"Very much so."

"What's her name again?"

"Denise," Adam replied.

"Tell us!" Ruby yelled. "Tell us what Diabolical Denise had to say!"

"What happened?"

"First off, she's so angry," Adam said. "Like vitriol-runs-through-her-veins angry. The kind of fury that eats a person alive from the inside out."

"Why's that?"

"First, because she was asked in for questioning. She kept yelling what an inconvenience it was and how we were wasting both of our time. She said she hadn't seen George in over a month."

"Did you believe her?"

Adam shrugged and finished his beer. "I don't know. She was pretty certain about it. But I kept wondering, was she upset because she's guilty of something, or just mad because she's been dragged into the investigation?"

"What did she say about their marriage?"

"She claimed George chose the church over her."

"That's what Ethel had told us," I said, then took a sip of my wine. "At least she didn't lie about that."

"But this felt... I don't know. Different," Adam said. "It was more than a relationship she wasn't satisfied with... instead, he hurt her at her core, down to her soul. When I interviewed her today, it was like she was at confession, spilling everything about her marriage, George, and what she lost because of him."

I stared at him, waiting for him to continue.

"They never had kids, and man, did she want them. But George didn't want to go through the IVF route after they tried for so long. She said it was almost a breaking point for them, but she stayed and lost her chance to become a mother because she loved George so deeply, she couldn't imagine her life without him."

"That wasn't really his fault," I said. "They wanted different things and she decided to stay. And you can't blame someone for infertility."

"Except, it *was* his fault," Adam replied. "He

had a vasectomy and never told her until after they divorced."

Ruby whistled and settled into a seat across the table. "Now, this is getting interesting."

"Oh, my," I whispered. "Okay, that's really dishonest."

"She never would've married him if she'd known. At least, that's what she says now."

"Can't blame her, especially if she wanted kids," I said.

"The way she explained it was she always put him first in the relationship, even giving up her own desires. He never did that for her. She was always second, especially to the church."

"So she left him."

"According to Denise, it took a long time for her to get to that place. She thought if she could become everything he wanted her to be, he'd finally see her... love her. She gained weight and lost weight. Grew her hair long, cut it short. Was quiet, then talkative. She tried so hard to figure out what he was looking for, what she should be in order to become first in his eyes, but she could never figure it out. The more she told me about her marriage, the angrier she became."

"That's really sad, Adam. Poor woman."

"I agree, but putting my pity aside, I have to wonder if she could've killed him."

"Out of spite? Or hatred? Like a crime of passion?"

"Exactly. She told me more than once he ruined her life, and he stole her best years."

"It's definitely plausible," I said, shrugging. "If she was that angry, then sure, I could see it happening."

Adam stared off into space for a few moments, the silence settling around us, along with the darkness of night.

"I've been giving us a lot of thought," he said after finishing off his beer.

"What about us?" Dread clawed at my chest. Was he going to break up with me?

"What our future looks like."

I poured another glass of wine, bracing myself. "Adam, you're worrying me. Please spit it out."

With a deep breath, he turned to me. "We came here to watch Darla and Jack get married. I don't think that's going to happen, but we'll see. Today, when I was listening to Denise recall her awful marriage, I tried to imagine being in a marriage like hers, and I can't fathom her pain. It made me reflect on our relationship. I think we're a good team. Do you?"

"Of course I do."

"You're the best thing that's happened to me," he said. "And I want to marry you."

His words came out rushed, as if he'd forced them.

My breath caught in my throat while my heart skipped a beat. "You do?"

"I do. And I don't want to wait. Listening to Denise today... she's a miserable woman, Bernie. All I could think was that I don't want to be like her, and I started examining my own life. What makes me happy? What doesn't?"

I stared at my wine, then at him, barely able to breathe. Adam wanted to marry me!

"And I came to the conclusion that you really make me happy," he said, grabbing my hand. "I want to be with you forever."

Somehow, I'd lost my ability to speak.

"I never imagined proposing to you this way. Instead, I thought it would be a big romantic gesture while we were out hiking, or at a nice restaurant. But I want us to be together. I want to be your husband and do my best to make you as happy as you make me. I want to be your number one and, well, you're already mine."

Oh, my word. *Adam wanted to marry me!* I kept repeating to myself.

"I was thinking we'd go down to the courthouse tomorrow. We don't even have to tell anyone. I don't want to steal Darla and Jack's moment if they do end up tying the knot on this trip. You and I can slip away and get married. We'll have a ceremony later that includes family, friends, tuxes, dresses and flowers... the whole bit. After listening to Denise today and how miserable she's been for so many years, I realized life's too short to be waiting for what I want. And I want you, Bernie."

"Holy cow," Ruby said. She was smiling when I glanced over at her. "My little granddaughter just had her first proposal."

And I still couldn't speak. Marriage? Tomorrow? What type of crazy idea was this? I'd never wanted a big, extravagant wedding, but a small intimate one always appealed to me. A courthouse? On a weekday morning? I wasn't sure how I felt about that.

Adam stared at me expectantly.

Did I want to marry him? Yes, I did. But did I want to do it at the courthouse?

"For Pete's sake, Bernie!" Ruby yelled. "Answer him! Don't leave the poor guy hanging!"

CHAPTER 14

THE NEXT MORNING, I curled my hair with shaky hands and slipped on the dress I had planned to wear to Darla's wedding—a purple sundress with a red cardigan and heels. Hopefully, I would be able to witness their nuptials, but for today, I'd be partaking in my own.

"You look beautiful, honey," Ruby said from the doorway. "You're glowing with happiness."

"Thanks," I said, running my hand down the front of my dress. "I can't believe we're doing this."

"I can. It's perfect. Just don't tell your mom."

"Right. She'd probably disown me if she knew I'd gotten married without her there."

"Probably. But it's okay, honey. If you want to

do this today, then do it. Don't fret over what your mother may or may not do."

I nodded and turned around. "Are you sure I look okay?"

"Prettier than a freshly picked peach," she said, smiling. "Say that quickly ten times. You'll be tripping all over your tongue."

"What do I say if one of the others sees me in this dress?" I asked.

Ruby shrugged. "Just tell them you felt like being beautiful today."

"Ready?" Adam said as he shut the door to our bedroom. "I was just downstairs and…" His words trailed off as our gazes met. "Wow, Bernie. You look so pretty."

"Thanks," I said, my cheeks heating as I studied him. Dressed in slacks and a blue button-down shirt that really brought out his eyes, he ran a hand through his blond hair. "You don't look too bad yourself."

As he took me into an embrace, he kissed my forehead. "Are you ready?"

Butterflies tickled my belly and my heart thundered. "I'm nervous and excited all at once, but yes, I'm ready."

"Let's go, then. I was just downstairs and the coast is clear. I think the others are sleeping off all the wine they drank last night."

"Then we better get moving."

"Woohoo!" Ruby shouted as I grabbed my purse. "Even though I'm dead, I get to see my granddaughter get married!"

Just as we hit the main floor, the bed and breakfast owner, Mandy, rounded the corner. "I thought I heard someone up and about," she said. "Good morning. Would you like some coffee?"

"No, thanks," Adam and I said in unison.

"You look very nice," she said. "Where are you off to?"

"We've got a meeting," Adam replied in his cop voice. No one ever questioned him when he used it, and Mandy simply smiled as we hurried to the front door.

While we drove to the courthouse, we held hands. My palms were a little sweaty, but I didn't have any doubts about marrying Adam. Every fiber of my being told me I'd made the right choice. Like he'd said, no one but us needed to know what we'd done, and we could plan a wedding ceremony at a later time when Darla and Jack weren't the center of attention.

Adam found a parking place down the street from Town Hall. Last night, we'd looked up their hours, and they opened their doors at nine. We arrived ten minutes early and hurried up the stairs to the door, which was still locked. I was so excited, I didn't even want or need any coffee.

The longest ten minutes of my life clicked by slowly. Adam and I were both jittery and paced the landing together.

"I can't believe we're going to do this," I said.

"Me neither. But it feels right, you know?"

"Yes. It does."

At one minute after nine, a portly woman with long black hair opened the door from the inside. "What can I do for you two?" she asked, her gaze grazing over us from head to toe. "Wait! Don't tell me. You want to get married!"

Adam and I exchanged glances and nodded.

"What a great way to start my day," she said. "Come on in."

"Excuse me," a man said, brushing by us inside. "Good morning, Clara."

"Morning, mayor."

Wait. *The mayor?* The same mayor related to Doug under the bridge and Buck, the ex-convict sharpshooter?

Of course, it made sense. We were at Town Hall, where his office would be located. I stared at him as he walked down the hallway and hung a right. A white shirt covered his broad shoulders, while his grey slacks hung a little long over his black loafers. His large bald spot gleamed under the hallway lights, but I hadn't gotten a look at his face. I fought the urge to hurry after him to question him about his son and Doug.

"Come on over here," Clara said. "I'll get you started on the paperwork."

We followed her to an office so small, I immediately felt claustrophobic. Adam and I took a seat while she walked behind a messy desk covered in stacks of manila folders and a computer. After pulling out a file from a drawer, she placed some papers onto a clipboard, grabbed the closest pen, and handed them to Adam.

"So, you're both over eighteen," she said. "That's a good start. Once the marriage license is issued, then you have up to one year to plan your wedding and get hitched."

Adam looked up from the paperwork. "We wanted to get married *today*," he said.

"We thought if we came down here, we'd be able to say our vows and marry," I chimed in.

Clara arched an eyebrow and shook her head. "I'll tell you what. Finish the paperwork, and I'll see what I can do."

She hurried from the room while Adam scribbled on the pages, stopping every now and then to question me on my information. Social security number? Year I was born?

"Well, at least he knows the day and month you were born, which is more than I could say for any of my husbands," Ruby said.

"You were never married," I whispered, glancing over at my ghost.

"I know, but it sure sounded good, didn't it?" she asked with a giggle. "Makes me appear worldly and experienced."

Adam finished the paperwork and grabbed my hand. "Dang it, Bernie. I'm so excited, I feel like I'm going to vibrate right out of my skin. This is totally the right thing to do."

I smiled and squeezed his fingers. "I feel the same way. I can't wait to be Bernadette Gallagher."

"You're going to take my last name?"

"I'd planned on it," I replied. "Did you not want me to?"

"Only if you want to," he said, leaning over to kiss me. "I'm just happy you agreed to this crazy plan."

Clara came back into the room and sat down behind her desk. "Usually, you need to make an appointment for this, but I called the minister.

He's coming over to do the honors. You two *will* be married today."

"Paul?" I asked, a sinking feeling settling in my stomach.

"Yes! Do you know him?"

"We've met," I said.

"Well, you actually think he could be a murderer," Ruby said. "Wouldn't that be something? He marries you today and Adam arrests him in the near future for killing someone. Not too many people can say they were married by a murderer. That's a story for the grandkids, Bernie."

I tried to imagine myself curled up on the couch in my old age, telling little ones that Grandpa and I had been married by a killer. No, it wasn't a good story at all.

"He's such a nice man," Clara said, sighing. "And so darn handsome!" She rummaged around in a drawer for something, then stood. "Be back in a flash. I'm missing my official stamper."

"Well, that should be interesting," Adam said under his breath when she'd left the room.

"Right? Do you think he'll marry one of the people who's investigating him?"

"I guess we'll find out."

When Clara returned, she had a cup of coffee

and her stamper. "Haven't had a chance to fuel up for my day yet." She looked over our paperwork, while nervous butterflies tickled my belly. A phone rang in another room. The sound of people talking down the hall filtered in, but I paid no attention to the conversation. I focused on the woman who was about to issue our marriage license.

"Looks good!" she said, picking up her stamp and slamming it down on the papers. "I'll collect the payment and you'll have your license to marry."

Adam fished out his wallet and took care of the fee.

"Paul mentioned he'd be right over," Carla said, running a hand through her hair. "Let me go see if I can catch him." Did she actually just suck in her gut as well?

"Carla's got the hots for old Minister Mayhem," Ruby said, snorting.

A few minutes later, Paul strode in, smiling, trailed by Carla, whose cheeks were red and her eyes shining with happiness as she stared at his back.

"Ah, Deputy Gallagher," Paul said, his grin fading a little. "I didn't know I'd be doing the honors of a man who is questioning me on the murder of a colleague."

"I didn't know either," Adam said, shaking his hand. "We would appreciate it if you could please do the ceremony."

Paul narrowed his gaze as he stared at me. "The woman from the parking lot. Where's your friend?"

"She's not here," I replied.

The minister nodded and sighed. "It would be very ungodly for me to hold a grudge toward you. Where are your witnesses?"

Adam and I traded glances. We had four of them sitting in the bed and breakfast who would've been happy to observe us being married, but we'd left them there.

"I'm a witness!" Ruby yelled. "I'm here!"

Pursing my lips together, I once again had a rush of utter sadness pulse through me. Ruby needed to be seen and heard and it broke my heart she wasn't.

"We didn't bring anyone," Adam said. "This was kind of a spur of the moment thing. We didn't know the rules."

"Then I can't marry you," Paul said, his smile firmly back in place, and I realized he enjoyed his upper hand.

"Can't we just get two people from the hallway?" I asked. "We don't care who the witnesses are."

He shrugged. "I don't see why not. Clara can't be one, though."

"I'll be right back," I said as I marched out the door into the hallway, more determined than ever to marry.

"You know, we should slip into the mayor's office," Ruby said. "We've got two suspects connected to him. I have a feeling he's in up to his elbows in George's death."

"Valid point," I muttered. "But later. Come hell or high water, I'm getting married today."

"Excuse me," I said to a woman my age waiting on a bench in the hallway. "I was wondering if you could witness my marriage."

She glanced at the closed doors to her right, then back at me while pushing her glasses up her nose. "I'm waiting for the city council meeting to start."

"It'll only be a few minutes," I said. "My boyfriend and I really want to get married today, but we didn't think about bringing witnesses."

She bit her lip and stared at the floor for a long moment, and I crossed my fingers behind my back. Finally, she said, "I suppose so. But I need to be at the meeting."

"Thank you." I sighed in relief. "I promise. No more than ten minutes. You can go right down the hall and I'll be just a minute."

"Who else are you going to corral?" Ruby asked.

The hallways were fairly empty, except for the staff. Just as I was about to grab someone off the street, Sam from the herbal store walked in. Dressed in a yellow sundress with her curly hair around her shoulders, she reminded me of a ray of sunshine.

"Hey," she said. "What are you doing here?"

"Getting married," I replied. "Could you please be a witness?"

She furrowed her brow then threw her head back and laughed. "What?"

After explaining my situation, she readily agreed.

We all gathered in Carla's small office, packed in like a bunch of sardines. Adam and I held hands, facing Paul. Sam's breath caressed the back of my neck while a drop of sweat trailed down Adam's cheek.

"It's hot in here," he whispered, wiping it away.

As Paul began the service, I tuned him out and stared at my soon-to-be-husband. My heart swelled with love as tears pricked my eyes. After a moment, Sam nudged me from behind, but I figured she accidently bumped me.

"Earth to Bernie!" Ruby yelled. "It's your turn!"

My turn to what?

"Say I do, Bernie!"

"I do," I whispered. Tears of happiness flooded down my cheeks as Adam kissed me.

And that was it. In a matter of minutes, I had become Mrs. Adam Gallagher.

"Excuse me," Paul said. "I have to see the mayor."

When he pushed out the door, Sam congratulated us, as did the woman who had been waiting for the council meeting to begin. Both left to get on with their business.

"You've got black tracks of mascara running down your face and snot coming out your nose," Ruby said, chuckling. "Go clean yourself up, honey."

"I'm going to the restroom," I said to Adam. "I'll be right back."

As I strode down the hallway following the

signs to the bathroom, I realized I was trailing Paul.

At a T in the hallway, he went to the left. The restrooms were to the right. I traded glances with Ruby.

"We need to see what he says to the mayor," Ruby said. "In my book, both are suspects and we have one heck of an opportunity here. You can freshen up in a minute."

I nodded and trailed Paul. At the end of the hall, he knocked on a door, then went in, slamming it behind him. Ruby and I rushed forward, and she disappeared into the office.

But she didn't need to because I heard everything loud and clear.

"I'm asking you again!" Paul yelled. "You wanted me here to do a job. I need my church open and the police off my back!"

CHAPTER 15

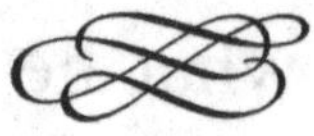

AN HOUR LATER, Adam, Ruby, and I walked along the Riverwalk. I tried to ignore my ghost, but as she hummed and spun in circles next to me while pointing out this bird, that tree, the guy in the waders across the river, my irritation grew. I wanted to spend time alone with my husband, but I couldn't because she and I were joined at the hip, especially outside the house. Resentment filled my heart, and I hated the emotion, but I couldn't brush it away, either.

"What do you think that meant?" I asked Adam referring to Paul's verbal assault on the mayor. As I pushed my purse strap up my shoulder again, I wished I'd left it at the bed and breakfast. The bag also added to my annoyance.

"I don't know," he said. "But it sure needs to be looked into. What job? Murdering George? Or building the mega church?"

"If he was brought here to kill George, then why didn't he just leave town afterward?"

"Because it makes him look guilty!" Ruby said. "Like he's running away from his dirty deeds!"

"It looks to me like the mayor is up to his eyeballs in this," I said, linking my arm through my husband's. How it tickled me to say that! "First, his bad apple son and then we still don't know how he's related to Doug, only that he is."

"I asked Mallory about that," Adam replied. "He's a cousin to the mayor."

"Hmm... it's still odd he wouldn't try to help him. He's family."

"You can't help people who don't want to be helped," Ruby said. "Sam told us he's perfectly happy living under the bridge."

Point taken. Just because living the way Doug did upset me to my core didn't mean he wasn't happy with it.

"We wouldn't allow him to camp out like that in Sedona unless we had direct orders from the mayor," Adam said. "My guess—the mayor has demanded he be left alone, but I'll ask Mallory next time I talk to her."

As we strolled along, a light breeze brushed my cheeks and ruffled my dress around my legs. The sun shone brightly, not a cloud visible through the tall trees. A perfect day to get married.

"Do you think our friends are wondering where we are and what we're up to?" I asked.

Adam chuckled and checked his phone. "Considering it's ten in the morning and they had so much wine, I'd say no. But Gunner's probably at the sheriff's office by now. I fully expect him to call at any moment and ask where I've been."

"I hope not," I replied. "I'd like to spend a little time with you before we have to get back to solving a murder."

As he turned to me, he took both my hands in his. "I was thinking about getting some rings. There's a jewelry store in town named Jemisphere. We could go there and poke around."

"But we don't want people to know we're married," I said. "I'd love to buy rings today, but everyone would notice them and ask questions. We didn't want to steal Darla and Jack's thunder."

Adam sighed as his phone rang. "I want to shout from the rooftops that we're hitched, but you're right. We need to think about Darla and Jack."

"Are you going to answer that?" I asked as the incessant ringing continued. "Maybe it's Gunner, as you predicted."

Adam pulled out the device from his pants pocket. It wasn't Gunner. Instead, Sheriff Bruce Walker's name scrolled across the screen. "I better take this." As he answered, his spine stiffened and his smile faded. "Hey, Sheriff. What can I do for you?"

I admired his jawline as he gazed out over the river listening to his boss. A light breeze tousled his blond hair. *My husband.* Holy cow, I couldn't get over the fact we'd taken the plunge and married. Or had we eloped? Yes, we had. Whatever we'd done, I was thrilled.

Ruby stood right next to Adam attempting to overhear the conversation. His brow furrowed and he stepped away from her. He probably had gotten the chills with her so close, or he could smell her distinct scent of lavender and marijuana. My grandmother placed her hands on her hips, glared at him, and moved in closer. She would not be denied her ghostly snooping rights.

After a few moments, Adam hung up and shoved the phone in his pocket. "Bruce is going to be here tomorrow to help out."

"Oh! Bruce-y Boy will be arriving!" Ruby squealed. "I've missed that sexy man!"

"Hopefully, a pair of fresh eyes on everything will lead you to the killer," I said, trying to brush off the disappointment of the sheriff's arrival. Could he help solve the murder? Yes, most definitely. Would it mean less time with Adam? Yes. And, yes, I was being very selfish, but we had just tied the knot.

"That would be nice," Adam said, wrapping his arm around my shoulder. "Do you think we should head back to the bed and breakfast, or should we try to grab some food at one of the restaurants?"

I glanced up ahead and realized we'd approached the bridge where Doug lived. I noted him sitting in the shadows. "Let's go see our bridge dweller and listen to what he has to say about the arrow we found on his pile of stuff."

Adam groaned but followed me. "My boss is going to be here tomorrow, Bernie. He's going to tie up all my time. Can we please go grab something to eat?"

"This will only take a minute," I said. "Then we can go find some breakfast." The opportunity to speak to Doug again was too good to pass up.

"Hey!" I said as we approached. "Hi, Doug! I was wondering if you had a minute to talk to us?"

As we walked into the shaded tunnel, his features became clearer. His gaze appeared bright, which I considered a good indicator that a productive conversation was possible.

"What about?" he asked, standing. "Do I know you?"

"Sort of?" I replied. "My friend and I were here a day or two ago."

He nodded and tapped the side of his head. "Right. I remember. What do you want?"

"Well, we were river rafting the other day and there was... an accident, I guess you could say. Someone was shooting arrows at our raft."

"Someone was trying to kill you all!" Ruby shouted, throwing her hands in the air with dramatic flair. "They wanted you all dead so you'd join me in this torturous limbo!"

"Really?" Doug asked, his eyes widening. "Why would they do that?"

"I'm not sure. We came by here after it happened and noticed an arrow on top of your pile." I pointed to his possessions.

"Where is it now?" he asked, glancing over at his stuff. "I don't remember seeing an arrow."

"We had to take it for physical evidence," Adam said. "A crime had been committed."

As he slowly turned back to us, I watched his features carefully and noted stark fear in his gaze. "Do you think I did it?"

I shook my head while Adam shrugged. "Did you?" he asked.

"N-no!" Doug shouted. "I'd never shoot anyone! I'm a pacifist!"

"We didn't think you did," I said, laying my hand on his tanned arm. "We just wanted to ask you some questions about it."

"This guy didn't shoot anything at anyone," Ruby said. "He's as harmless as a dead mouse."

With all the diseases rodents carried, I considered them somewhat dangerous, dead or alive, but I wouldn't argue the point. Based on what I'd seen for myself and heard from Sam at Sage Advice, I didn't think Doug was guilty, either. However, I did believe he could give us a clue or two, even if he wasn't aware of it.

With a long sigh, he sat down on his chair. "Then you'll leave? You're making me nervous."

"I promise," I said, once again feeling overwhelming pity for the man.

Adam and I both crouched down against the opposite wall and I took a really hard look at

Doug's home. Besides the pile of stuff, the area was quite clean. I noted an old, broken broom leaning against his possessions and decided he must use it regularly. I'd seen houses with more dust than his tunnel. Not mine, though, of course.

"Despite him living under a bridge, this place is spotless," Ruby said. "I don't think my house ever looked this good until you moved in, Bernie."

"You're related to Buck and the mayor. Correct?" Adam asked.

Doug nodded. "Unfortunately, yes."

"Why do you say that?" I asked.

"I don't like either one of them," he said, shrugging. "But I have to kiss my cousin's butt so he keeps the police off my back."

Well, at least we had that question answered. Mallory and her deputies ignored Doug because of the mayor.

"When was the last time you saw Buck?" Adam asked.

"Probably right after he got out of prison," Doug replied. "Whenever that was."

"A month ago," I offered, recalling Tricia sharing the fact.

"I lose track of time," he said. "Days run into each other."

Not surprising. I was dead sober a good portion of the time and I had trouble keeping track of my days. But high on drugs? Forget it. "Do you know who the arrow belongs to?" I asked.

Adam's phone rang. Without glancing at the screen, he reached into his pocket and silenced it, his concentration on the homeless man.

"You could've answered," Doug said. "Not a problem for me."

"I'm more interested in hearing what you've got to say. We could've been hurt or killed on the rafting ride, so it's important to me I find out who shot the arrows and why." He pointed at me. "I just married her and I can't imagine my life without her. If someone is trying to hurt my new bride, I need to know who it is so I can put a stop to it."

"Did you two really just tie the knot?" Doug asked. "As in, *today*?"

I smiled and glanced at my phone. "About forty-five minutes ago. Paul married us."

He shook his head. "I'm happy for you guys, but I wish George could've married you. I didn't like him much, but Paul's worse."

"Why is that?" I asked.

"Because he wants to change everything about this town. We are not a mega church community.

I, for one, don't want the current church flattened, but I don't have much of a say. If I had to choose between George and Paul, I'd choose George any day, even if he couldn't mind his own business."

Interesting. He'd made it clear George wasn't one of his favorite people and now claimed Paul was worse? The good-looking minister must be an ugly human being.

"And if he did tear down our old church in order to build his new, modern church, he'd have to buy the buildings around him," Doug continued, obviously having given the situation a lot of thought. "They'd be gone as well. There's too much history in those old places."

"Like what?" I asked.

"Well, the church was once a Catholic one, even though it's non-denominational now. They kept everything intact from when it had been built a hundred years ago. The building on the right, Knit Wit, used to be an orphanage. Next to Knit Wit... that was once a brothel. Can you imagine the uproar when the brothel opened up down the street from the church?" He shook his head. "I have a book on the history of Heywood if you'd like to borrow it. You can give me something as collateral... so I make sure you bring it back."

"That's nice of you," Adam said. "But we're more interested in getting back to the arrow. If it wasn't yours, can you tell me who it belonged to?"

"Nope."

"Why not?" Ruby said. "Does he know and he's not telling us or is he totally in the dark?"

I wasn't sure myself. "Can you elaborate on that? Do you know who the arrow belonged to?"

"Maybe," Doug replied. "But I can't remember right now."

Huh? Did he know who the arrow belonged to or not?

"What would make you recall a name?" Adam asked.

"My guess is some cold, hard cash," Ruby said. "Slip him a few bills, Bernie."

Adam rose to his feet and pulled out his wallet. "Will twenty help your memory?"

Doug gave a shrug. "Well, it's becoming a little clearer."

"Thirty?" Adam said, glaring at the homeless man, irritation biting in his voice.

"That should do it."

While Adam handed over the bills, I wasn't sure what to think. As a police officer, should he be bribing people for information that may or may not be true? I'd have to ask him about the ethics of this situation later.

"Who does the arrow belong to?" Adam asked. "And no more screwing around."

Doug laughed and waved the money away. "I'm just messing with you. I don't want your money. It's the root of all evil."

I narrowed my gaze on the funny man, not sure I agreed because I liked money just fine and found nothing evil about it.

"Who does the arrow belong to?" Adam asked again, stuffing the bills back into his wallet.

"Your husband is about two seconds away from losing his cool," Ruby said. "I wonder what happens then? Does he beat the snot out of old Dougy boy here?"

"What color was it?" Doug asked.

"Red." All three of us answered in unison.

"I know two people who can hit a moving raft on the river," Doug said.

"And their names are?" Adam said through gritted teeth.

"One is my nephew, Buck. He's a sharp-shooter. The other is his daddy."

"The mayor?" Ruby yelled. "The mayor's

pinging rafts with arrows? What kind of tourist department is he running?!"

"And the mayor's always shot red arrows since he was a boy," Doug continued. "Said it was his signature while competing."

CHAPTER 16

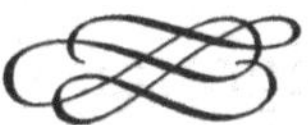

AFTER OUR TALK WITH DOUG, Adam's phone continued to ring. When he finally answered, he was called into the sheriff's office. Gunner stopped by and picked him up while Ruby and I made our way toward Town Hall so I could fetch the car.

"How does it feel to be someone's old lady?" she asked.

I rolled my eyes, my thoughts not on my marriage, but on our conversation with Doug and George's murder.

"Do you think the mayor has something to do with killing George?" I murmured as we strolled along. "I mean, I feel like there are two different things going on here. Someone died, and someone was shooting arrows. I'm confused on how they all fit together."

"Well, maybe you all are asking too many questions about the murder and someone wants to off you."

"Maybe," I said, sighing. I stopped and crossed my arms over my chest, glancing around and hoping no one was paying me much attention while I held a conversation with an entity they couldn't see. "How are we going to prove the mayor had anything to do with the rafting incident, let alone a murder?"

A slow smile turned my ghost's lips upward. "Oh, I have a plan for that."

"Oh, no."

"Oh, yes."

"Maybe we should just go to the sheriff and tell her what Doug said."

Ruby sighed and shook her head. "She's doing the mayor's bidding, Bernie. If he says he didn't have anything to do with it, then she's going to believe him. Use your noggin, girl. It's a dead end."

"I'm not sure what to do, then," I said, biting my thumbnail.

"Bernie, we follow my plan."

"That always leads to me almost being killed

or thrown into prison!" I said. "Your plans are the absolute worst."

"Oh, come on. They aren't that horrible."

"I was almost dropped down a stairwell head-first and given enough drugs to knock out a horse," I said. "Yes, I could've died. Not to mention all the times I could've gone to jail for breaking and entering and being on property I shouldn't have been on."

"Are you finished?" Ruby asked. "Are you ready to hear my epic idea?"

I sighed and glanced out over the river. There were too many questions swirling around for me to do nothing. Maybe I'd just *listen* to what Ruby had to say. "I suppose so."

"Good. Now, pay attention."

~

"He'll never go for it," I said as we drove back to the bed and breakfast. "Never."

"Mr. Dimples is a hardened criminal! He needs the rush of breaking the law in order for his heart to keep beating. He's not a settle-down-and-mow-the-yard guy. Trust me on this one!"

Was she correct on her assessment of Jack? He was the one who was supposed to be married this week. Marriage didn't necessarily equate mowing a lawn, but I understood the reference.

Just as we turned up the street toward the bed and breakfast, Darla and Jezebel slowed their car and I rolled down my window. "Drive! Drive! They'll trap you into something other than our plan!" Ruby shouted.

But I couldn't simply pass my friends, so I stopped.

"Where are you two off to?" I asked.

"We're going into town for a little shopping," Jezebel said. "Hopefully, a little retail therapy will kill off this wine headache."

"Come with us, Bernie!" Darla said.

I gave it a half-second thought. Shopping would be wonderful, but then Ruby yelled, "No! Don't! This is our chance to get Jack alone!"

Of course, she was right. A murder to solve and a mayor to bust—hopefully, an all-in-one big swoop of highly illegal activity. "I think I'll pass for now, but thanks!" Pulling away, I smiled and waved, leaving no room for further discussion.

After we parked and hurried into the house, I glanced around the living room for Jack.

"Hi, there," Richard, the owner, said as he emerged from the kitchen, wiping his hands with a dishtowel. "Can I get you anything?"

"No, thanks. I was looking for Jack."

"He's outside having some coffee and ibuprofen."

"Thanks."

Ruby and I rushed through the house to the back door to find the man right where Richard had said: sitting at the picnic table with a cup of coffee.

"Hey, Jack," I said, sitting down across from him. "How're you feeling?"

"Like a truck ran me over," he said.

"Hello, Mr. Dimples," Ruby purred, sidling up next to him. "Aren't you looking good enough to eat today?"

"Is she near me?" he asked as he shivered. "I feel like she's right here."

"Oh, I am, sweet cheeks," Ruby said. "I'm so close I can lick your cute little dimples."

"She's next to you," I said, closing my eyes so I didn't have to witness Ruby's tongue caressing Jack's cheek.

"What's she saying?" he asked.

"Oh, nothing," I replied while Ruby licked him again. "You aren't feeling well, then?" Maybe if I pushed the conversation in a different direction, Ruby would stop with her antics.

"Yeah," he replied, sighing. "I don't even like wine. Why in the heck did I drink so much?"

I only hoped he didn't feel so awful that he wouldn't want to join me in Ruby's plan. "So… what are you up to today?"

"Nothing," he said. "I'm actually a bit bored. Shopping doesn't sound good, and frankly, I'm ready to go home."

"What about marrying Darla?" I asked.

"This trip has been such a pain, I'd be fine going to the courthouse in Sedona." He shrugged. "The dress, the church—none of that ever mattered to me. Only Darla. I just want us to be married."

"I'm sorry, Jack," I said. "This trip has been a nightmare."

"Yes. But it is what it is. Darla's still convinced the killer will be found and we'll be married tomorrow."

"What do *you* think?"

"I don't know," he said. "Like I mentioned, I really don't care at this point."

Biting my tongue, I fought the urge to reveal my own secret marriage. Instead, I focused on recruiting Jack for Ruby's plan.

"I may be able to help you get one step closer to marrying her tomorrow," I said, lowering my voice as I glanced around. Our hosts didn't need to hear my law-breaking scheme.

"What did you have in mind?" Jack asked. "The church won't open until the killer's caught."

Leaning forward, I whispered, "I think I know who shot at the raft. And, he also may be the murderer."

"But you could be wrong on that," Ruby said.

"I'm not sure if the person shooting arrows at us is the same as the killer, but they may be," I said. "Or I could be totally wrong. However, I'm pretty certain I know who shot at the raft. I just need to prove it."

"How do you plan on doing that?" Jack asked.

"Well, I need your help."

Jack narrowed his gaze on me and quickly glanced around the yard. "What do you want me to do?"

"Put your skills from your former life to work."

He didn't flinch but took another drink of his coffee. After a moment he said, "You want me to burglar someone's home or office?"

"Yes. It's a house."

"Whose?"

"Does it matter?" I asked, shrugging. I really didn't want him to know I intended on breaking into the home of probably the most important man in town.

"It does," he said, leaning toward me. "Because the more clout someone has, the more influence they have. If I'm going to break into Mr. Joe No-Name's house, that's one thing. But if I'm burgling someone important, that's a whole other ball of crap I'm not sure I want to bounce around."

"Fair enough," I said. "The mayor."

His eyes widened and he straightened in his seat. "You want to break into the mayor's house?"

"Bingo, Hot Stuff!" Ruby yelled as I nodded.

"Are you drunk?" he asked, taking another sip of coffee and shaking his head. "If not, you've lost your marbles."

"No, I'm not drunk," I replied, just slightly offended. After all, it *was* a crazy plan. "We can do it like last time. You just get me a door open and I'll go in and find what I'm searching for."

"What *are* you looking for?"

"Matching arrows to the one that hit our raft," I said. "Perhaps the bow that launched it."

Jack snorted. "You'll need more than that to put someone away."

"Yes, but it's a start. And, if the mayor is involved in the murder that ruined your wedding, maybe I can find something that will tie him to it."

While he sipped his coffee, his gazed darted all around the yard.

"I can practically see that hamster wheel spinning in there, Mr. Stud Muffin," Ruby said. "He's debating the intelligence of this idea. Is it smart? Probably not. Is it safe? Heck, no. Does he want to be involved? My guess is yes. He likes the unsafe part… the danger. The rush of breaking into the freaking mayor's house—"

"Okay, I'm in," he said. "But we do this my way. You and your ghost are just along for the ride."

"I'll ride off with you into any sunset, you luscious hunk," Ruby purred.

"It's a deal," I said. "You're in charge."

He nodded and set down his coffee cup. "You aren't going to tell Darla about this either, right?"

"Nope," I held up my right hand. "I swear, this secret is safe with me."

"Good."

"Have you told her about your former life?" I asked. "About your prison stint?"

"Yeah, I did."

"How did she react to hearing about it?"

"About as well as I could expect from a straitlaced good girl," Jack said, chuckling. "Thankfully, I was able to convince her I was no longer that man."

"But you are that man, my beautiful beefcake," Ruby cooed, blowing in his ear. "Bad to the bone. Just the way I like them."

"Oh, for goodness' sake," I hissed while goosebumps appeared on Jack's neck. "Knock it off, Ruby."

She cackled as she moved away from him and he rubbed the side of his face.

"What was she doing?" he asked. "I felt a cool breeze."

"Just… just being Ruby," I replied with a huff. Sometimes, that dang ghost of mine drove me nuts with her inappropriate behavior, and I found myself wanting to apologize to Jack, but then I remembered he couldn't hear or see her. She still embarrassed me.

"When do we do this?" he asked.

"Today?"

"Seriously? When?"

"How about now?"

He pursed his lips. "You come up with some crazy stuff. You know that?"

I didn't bother to point out it was Ruby's idea, but I nodded anyway.

"Do we know where he lives?" Jack asked.

After pulling out my phone, I realized I didn't even know the mayor's name. Once I googled that—Jeffrey Ricker—finding his address was easy. In fact, I located an article in the local paper about a community Easter egg hunt that had taken place two years ago on his property. In the photo, he was smiling at the camera, his wife, and a younger Buck at his side. The piece also mentioned his wife working in a local accountants' office. Google produced a map for me, and we were ready to go.

"We're set," I said, standing. I picked up my bag and once again threw it over my shoulder. "I just need to change my clothes. Are you ready?"

Jack nodded. "We'll have to stop by the hardware store before we do anything. I need to pick up a few things."

CHAPTER 17

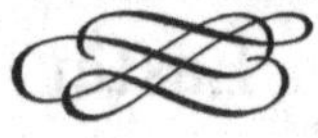

WE PARKED down the street from the house and walked past it. No cars in the driveway, which was an excellent sign. I called the accountants' office and asked if Betty Ricker was working, and when they transferred me to her desk, I quickly hung up. The mayor would surely be toiling away at Town Hall—he ran the dang place.

"Stay here," Jack said. "I'll call you if the coast is clear."

I stood on the corner of the street while attempting to hide behind a tree but appear casual at the same time. Like I belonged. After pulling out my phone, I looked in the direction Jack had gone, out of the corner of my eye, while pretending to study my screen. Ruby hooted and hollered while playing chicken with the odd car passing by. I had to admit, she had pretty good timing, jumping out of the way just in the nick of time, and I couldn't help but wonder if she had practiced while alive. I wouldn't put it past her.

The longer I waited for the call, the more tension built up within me, and the more I worried about things that had yet to happen. What if Jack never phoned and went into the house without me? What if he got caught? How would I explain his arrest and my complicity to Darla?

When my phone buzzed in my hand, I almost dropped it.

"Be careful, butterfingers," Ruby said.

"It's Jack," I murmured. Sighing with relief, I answered. "Hi."

"No one's home," he growled without preamble. "Walk quickly, but don't draw attention to yourself and hurry up."

I hurried down the street with Ruby in tow.

"You're waddling like a duck with a stick up its butt," she said. "You don't look ordinary in the least bit. If I lived in this neighborhood and noticed you from my window, I'd laugh and call my neighbors to tell them to take a gander outside at the woman walking like a duck with a stick up its butt."

I slowed my stroll and tried to allow my hips to roll naturally.

"That's a little better. Quack. Quack."

As a car drove by, I lowered my head and wished my hair wasn't in a ponytail. When down, it provided a nice curtain to hide my face.

I glanced around for Jack when I arrived at the house. Not seeing him, I wondered if he was already inside. Should I go in? Had he left the door open for me? Or should I knock? After a moment, I located him at the side of the house. He waved me over and I followed him around back.

"We have one problem," he said as we approached the sliding glass door. "There's a dog inside, but I don't think he's dangerous. He doesn't look like it, anyway."

Uh oh. I wasn't going to risk a dog attacking us.

The big, golden beauty stared at us through the glass, his tail wagging, and I laughed. "It's a Golden Retriever," I said. "Aren't they usually harmless?"

"Oh, what a sweet boy," Ruby said. "I'll take care of this big, golden ball of fluff."

After she ghosted through the window, the dog became more excited and focused all his attention on her. She sat down on the floor and began to stroke the sides of his face while he kissed her. Seconds later, he'd rolled over to his back and she rubbed his tummy.

"We're good to go," I said. Ruby definitely had a way with animals.

"Is your ghost in there?" Jack asked, pulling his tools from his pocket and began to jimmy the lock.

"Yes. She's giving him belly rubs."

Jack snickered as the lock popped. "I didn't see any alarm system when I cased the place, so I think we're good."

"I'll take it from here," I said. "You don't have to go in."

"No, I'm with you, Bernie. If this ship sinks, we go down together."

With a nod, I stepped inside, actually feeling a little better I had a partner in crime who wasn't dead.

I held my hand out and noted the nervous shaking. My first time breaking and entering had been into Adam's condo. I was intimately familiar with it. The surge of fear and adrenaline coursing through me as I entered the new space had my stomach rolling to the point where I wondered if I was going to be sick.

Sweat dotted my brow and my chest constricted as I tried to take some deep breaths and calm myself.

"Come on," Jack whispered. "And be on the lookout for cameras. Some people have them set up so they can watch their dogs during the day."

Or in Adam's case, carefully track where his ghost hid his stuff. If I set up cameras in my house, all I'd see was Elvira sprawled out on the couch or in a sunbeam. All things considered, my cat was boring... except when she decided to destroy Christmas trees.

As we snuck through the kitchen into the living room, I admired the muted shades of green, tan, and yellow. Pushing the thoughts aside, I tried to think of where someone would store their bows and arrows. A closet? The garage? Under a bed? An attic or basement? I certainly didn't notice anything in the living room.

"We'll quickly check each room," Jack said. "Then move out into the garage."

Too frightened to answer, I followed him into the first bedroom. With the simple furniture, lack of decorations, and old quilt covering the bed and a layer of dust on the dresser, I figured it was obviously a guest room. I dropped to my knees to explore under the mattress while Jack rummaged through the closet. Our search took less than thirty seconds.

Ruby appeared in the doorway with the dog. "You guys are moving too far away from me," she said. "And according to his tags, this is Biscuit, by the way. He's the best boy ever." She leaned over and kissed his snout. With Ruby only being able to move fifteen feet away from me while out of our house, she'd definitely remain close.

"Next room," Jack said, motioning me to follow.

The bedroom didn't feel lived in, despite having some posters on the wall, a red comforter, and knickknacks on the desk. Probably Buck's old room while growing up. The closet had been packed with stuff, as well as the space under the bed. Jack and I moved things around a little while we searched. I rifled through the drawers and sighed in frustration.

"Nothing," he murmured.

We hurried into the master bedroom, which was neat and tidy. It didn't take us long to go through everything, and once again we found zilch.

Biscuit panted as he watched our search. Ruby stood at his side and pet his head.

"Garage?" I asked.

Jack nodded and we slowly opened the door leading from the house to the garage. No cars, but plenty of shelving packed with miscellaneous stuff. As we searched, I kept glancing at the automatic door to the outside, wondering what we'd do if it suddenly began opening. If that were the case, someone was on their way home and we'd be busted.

"Ruby," I hissed. "Go outside and watch for anyone pulling up. I'll stand near this end of the garage so you can stay there until Jack's done."

"Aye aye, Captain!" she cried out, then turned to the dog. "You need to stay here, my furry friend. Don't bite anyone, okay?"

I stood in place while Jack looked through all the shelves. "Are you sure about this, Bernie?" he asked. "There's no sign of bows, arrows or anything that shoots."

"I don't know," I whispered. "I thought we'd find something to at least tie him to the rafting accident."

"That wasn't an accident," Jack said, pointing at me. "We could've died."

"You're right."

"Mayday! Mayday!" Ruby shouted from out front. "Incoming! Incoming!"

Jack and I exchanged panicked glances and

hurried into the house. Biscuit trotted behind us, his tail wagging.

As the garage entry squeaked and Jack quietly shut the door, I spun around in a circle. "What do we do? What do we do?" I hissed. "How do we get out?"

"The backdoor!" Ruby yelled. "Run for your life! The backdoor!" I turned and hurried down the hallway while Biscuit barked behind me. He must have thought we were playing because he quickly jumped in front of me, sending me sprawled out onto the beige carpet. As he licked my face, Jack grabbed my arm and pulled me upright.

"Oh, heck!" Ruby screamed. "They're inside!"

We'd never make it to the backdoor.

Immobile with panic, I glanced at Jack. Gone was the fun sparkle in his eye I usually saw there. Instead, I noted cool calculation as his gaze darted around. A split second later, he pulled me over to a closet near the front door I hadn't noticed before just as the backdoor slammed shut and voices filtered down the hall. Biscuit trotted over and jumped at the wooden panel as Jack shut us in. Surrounded by coats, boots and a basket full of gloves and hats, we had mere inches separating us. Jack brought his finger up to his lips, motioning me to be quiet. As the cramped space closed in around me, I felt like I couldn't breathe. Instead, I shut my eyes and leaned my forehead on Jack's chest.

"Come here, Biscuit," Ruby said, her voice gentle. "Come see me." At least she was working on distracting the dog.

"When I tell you to get the heck out of there and head out the front door, do it," Ruby said. "In the meantime, I'll keep Biscuit away from you."

Two men entered the living room. I'd heard the voices before, but I couldn't quite place them.

"It's Buck and that kid from the coffee shop," Ruby said. "The wannabe Fabio."

I hadn't been aware the two were acquainted but it was a small town, so I shouldn't be surprised.

"Help yourself to a soda," Buck said. "I hid the weed in my bedroom. I'll go pull it out."

We hadn't found any marijuana during our search. "Clutch move keeping it in your parents' house," Fabio called. "Too smart, dude!"

"Barista Boy is coming this way!" Ruby yelled. "Buck's in his bedroom! Don't make a sound!"

I pictured her sitting right outside the door with the dog.

"Dude!" the barista called. "I think your dog

has been into the ganga! He totally smells like that and flowers!"

"That stupid mutt better not have been in my stash," Buck said. *Oh, my word. He was right outside the door!*

"Don't worry, Bernie!" Ruby called. "If they try to open that door, they'll have to get through me first!"

Which wouldn't be very difficult, considering she was a ghost.

"I'll smack them over the head with a lamp!" she continued. "One! Two! They'll never know what hit 'em!"

"Biscuit's not usually this calm," Buck said. "My parents are nicer to this dog than they ever were to me."

"They're petting Biscuit," Ruby said. "I don't know how you two are going to get out of this one. I think I may have to kill them both."

"Did you see the look on Harold's face today?" Buck asked. "When I asked him about the rafting accident?"

Wait. Harold. The owner of the rafting company?

"I did," Mr. Hair Swinger said. "Do you think he knows you did it?"

"Does it matter? He's going down. I'll ruin his business."

"It seems like you should just open your own rafting company and see what happens," Fabio said. "Play fair, you know?"

"Playing fair is for mere mortals," Buck said. "To rise to the top, you have to get dirty."

Holy cow. Jezebel had been right. The arrows hadn't been aimed at my friends and me, but at the raft itself. And man, did that kid have a lot to learn in life, unless he was shooting to be a politician. Then I could understand his reasoning.

"They'll catch you one way or the other," the barista said.

"No, they won't. I used my father's arrow and left it with Dirty Doug down by the river. If those idiots at the police department figure out it's there, they'll think he did it. Maybe then they'll clean out his trash."

"He's not a bad guy," Fabio said. "And who's to say they won't nail your dad?"

"Because he's the freaking mayor! He runs this Podunk town and they won't touch him. They'll bury it."

It seemed Buck had thought of everything.

"Let's go smoke down by the river," he said. "I

don't want my parents coming home and catching me here."

"Right on," barista boy said, their voices fading as they walked down the hallway toward the garage again.

When I heard the door slam, I sighed and opened my eyes. Claustrophobia still had me in its grasp as I pushed the door open and inhaled fresh air. I realized I had felt like I was deep underwater, my lungs about to burst. Exiting the cramped space was me breaking the surface, finally able to breathe again.

"At least we solved the mystery of the rafting incident," Jack said, stepping out and leaning over to pet Biscuit.

"But how do we prove it?" I asked.

"Well, we've got an arrow that matches the one shot into the raft," Jack replied.

"No, we don't."

He turned back to the closet. "Yes, we do," he said, pulling one out. "They were behind the basket of gloves and hats."

Buck had the guts to try to take down another man's business in an awful, backhanded way. But did he have it in him to kill someone?

CHAPTER 18

As Jack and I drove away from the mayor's neighborhood, my phone rang. I pulled it out of my pocket and saw it was Adam calling. After what I'd just done, I didn't have the will to speak to him. My heart raced, sweat rolled down my back, and throwing up still seemed like a great idea.

"You better answer or he's going to wonder what's going on," Jack said.

"I can't," I whispered. "I need to calm down and we need to get our story straight. How are we going to explain the arrow and where it came from? And overhearing Buck? How do we bring all this to Adam's attention without telling him we broke the law?"

"You should've thought of that before you went into the house," Ruby said.

Glancing over my shoulder, I shot her a hard glare. "This *was* your idea."

"Oh, I know that," she replied. "And I'll gladly take credit where it's due. However, it was up to you to figure out how to use the information that you gathered, honey."

I faced forward and slammed my left hand against the dashboard. As I stared at it, I realized I should have a ring on. I was married. There wouldn't be any lying to Adam. Instead, I'd be dead honest with him and let him decide how to use the information. "I'm going to tell him everything," I said.

"Tell Adam everything?" Jack confirmed.

"Yes. But I'll leave you out of it. I'll just tell him Ruby and I are the conniving thieves."

"Are you sure?" Jack asked.

"I'm sure. I'm not going to put your relationship with Darla in jeopardy. If you want to come clean yourself, then that's up to you."

"Okay, I think I'll probably stay in the shadows on this one," Jack said. "Darla wasn't too happy with me when I told her about my past. It's best not to mention it's present in my future."

I glanced over at him as he drove. A small grin

crept across his face and at that moment, I realized Ruby had been right. "You like it, don't you? The adrenaline rush? The idea of being caught?"

When he chuckled, I couldn't help but smile as well.

"See?" Ruby said. "I told you Mr. Dimples had a slice of rotten in him."

"I guess you're right," Jack said. "Sometimes, I look at my life now—which is fantastic, don't get me wrong—but I remember the excitement of my prior life."

"Do you think you'd still be playing the burglar game if you hadn't been caught?" I asked.

"I don't know, Bernie," he said, shrugging. "In a way, I'm really glad they did catch me. Otherwise, I'd never have left the area and found Darla. I was never this happy before."

"That's really sweet," I said, leaning my head against the headrest. Suddenly, exhaustion overtook me and I shut my eyes, trying to figure out how I was going to finesse the story so I could share with Adam what we'd discovered.

When we arrived, I jolted to full consciousness as Jack turned off the car. The sun had almost set and I realized what a very long day I'd had. A marriage and a break-in. Not every day could be considered that exciting.

"Looks like everyone is here," Jack said. "Where are we going to say we went?"

"How about that we went into town to grab a quick bite to eat?"

"Sounds good. At the coffee shop?"

"Yes." We stared at each other a long moment and I smiled. "Thanks for your help today."

"No problem, Bernie. Let's just not make it a regular habit, okay?"

"Trust me, if I never burglar another house again, I'll be just fine."

"Let's leave the arrow in here," he said, and I agreed.

We exited the car and headed up to the house. Richard and Mandy greeted us warmly and directed us toward where we could find our friends. "I think Adam just went upstairs," Mandy said. "And Darla is in back with Gunner and Jezebel."

After thanking our hosts, Jack and I traded glances then headed our separate ways. Climbing the staircase reminded me of scaling a mountain. By the time I got to the top, I was ready for bed, even though it was dinnertime.

I opened our bedroom door and found Adam sitting on the bed, texting on his phone.

"Hey!" he said, standing. "How's my wife?"

"Good," I said, almost falling into his arms. "I have something to tell you."

"What's that?"

"Can we sit down?"

"Of course." He took my palm and led me over to the bed.

When we were seated, I grabbed his hands in mine, took a deep breath, and met his gaze.

"This is serious," he said, studying my face as his smile faded.

I nodded.

"Please don't tell me you don't want to be married anymore."

I burst out laughing and all the stress of the day flooded out of me. Here I was worried about admitting a crime, and my husband was concerned I didn't want to be married to him.

Tears tracked down my face and I wiped them away with my fingertips. Maybe this would be easier and go much more smoothly than I had anticipated. "Adam, marrying you was the best thing I've ever done. It's not that."

"What's going on then?"

"I did something today I shouldn't have," I said. "You'll probably be upset with me."

"Uh oh. What did you do?"

After taking a deep breath, I blurted out, "I broke into the mayor's house."

My husband stared at me slack jawed a long moment, his eyes wide. "You did what?"

"Remember how Doug told us the mayor always used red arrows?"

"Yes."

"I thought if I could find one in his house, the police could match them and at least someone would be arrested for shooting at the rafts, and maybe I could find a correlation between the shooter and the murderer, if they were one and the same."

Adam stood, rubbed his forehead with his thumb, and began pacing. "I'm not going to lecture you on how what you did is wrong. You aren't dumb."

"Thank you. You're right. I know what I did wasn't legal or morally correct."

He nodded and took a deep breath before sitting down. "Would you care to explain how this all went down?"

Was it lying if I omitted certain details, like Jack helping me? It didn't matter. I had promised him I would leave his name out of it.

"Well, I went over there—just Ruby and me. The sliding glass door in back was open, so we went in. Ruby played with the dog while I searched the house."

"And did you find anything nailing the mayor for the rafting incident?"

"Well, hang on a second," I said. "There's a little more to the story."

"Oh, man," Adam muttered, running his hand through his hair. "What's that?"

"Buck came in," I continued. "With a guy who works at the coffee shop."

"Does Buck live there?"

"I don't think so, but I'm not sure. He has a room there, but it didn't look lived in. More like his parents have preserved it for posterity or something."

"What did you do when the two men entered the house?"

"I hid in a closet," I replied. "That's where I found an arrow that matches the one we found on Doug's pile of stuff, and the bow to go with it."

Adam let out a long, slow whistle. "So, the mayor shot at the raft?"

"No," I said, shaking my head. "I overheard the conversation between Buck and the coffee kid. Buck did it."

"Why?"

"He wants to open up his own rafting company and he said he's taking out the competition before he does so."

Adam sighed and sat down again, placing his elbows on his knees and his head in his hands. I sensed the irritation rolling off him, and I hoped he didn't become too upset with me, no matter how much I deserved it.

I cleared my throat. "Buck said he left the arrow with Doug's stuff because he hoped the police would eventually find it and arrest him."

"What if they traced it back to the mayor?" Adam asked. "He competes with red arrows. They've been his signature since he was a kid! That has to be common knowledge in this town."

"According to Buck, it wouldn't matter because the police always do his father's bidding."

"So, the little turd gets off scot free for almost killing us," Adam muttered. As he sat upright, he clenched his fists. "He's willing to throw a family member under the bus so he gets free reign over the rafting business in town. Unbelievable. Whatever happened to working hard and being better than your competition?"

"I wondered the same thing. Buck has shown himself to be an entitled little brat," I said. "I guess some things don't change, even with prison time."

"I'm not sure what to do with this information," Adam said. "I can't go to the sheriff with it because then I'll have to explain how I got it."

"It may not matter anyway," I said. "If it came out publicly that Buck had shot the arrows, the mayor would probably put an end to any investigation. It sounds like Sheriff Mallory Richards is far more interested in covering for the mayor than searching for justice."

"You're probably right." Adam glanced over at me. "So, the mayor's back door was just open?"

I nodded, but my cheeks warmed.

"You're turning pink," Ruby said, rolling her eyes. "It's a dead giveaway you're being dishonest."

With a grin, he said, "You're lying, but I don't want to know any more about your afternoon adventure."

"I have the arrow in the car if you decide to take it to the sheriff."

"Wait a minute," Adam said. "Were you with Jack?"

"Oh, man. You're so busted," Ruby murmured.

"I-I was later today. I broke into the mayor's place earlier."

"Oh, really?"

"Yes."

"I don't believe that, either. I think Jack was

with you while you were pretending to be Betty Burglar."

"No, he—"

"Bernie, don't lie, okay?"

"You're kind of trapped now," Ruby admonished. "Better own up to it. Just make sure he doesn't tell Darla."

"Please, don't say anything to Darla," I begged. "She'll be upset with Jack if she finds out what he's been doing today."

"My lips are sealed," he said, grabbing his ringing phone from the nightstand. "It's Mal."

After a quick greeting, he listened intently, then fell back on the mattress and closed his eyes. "Thanks for letting me know," he said, hanging up.

"What is it?"

"The coffee came back clean," he said. "It didn't contain the poison."

"So it must have been the salad," I said. "The lab work on that should be back soon."

"She never had it done," Adam groaned, rubbing his face. "She thought it was the coffee so she concentrated on that. I just hope that whatever was in that salad hasn't broken down."

"Why in the world wouldn't she have the salad

tested?" I asked. "How could she mess this up so badly?

"Because she's never worked a murder," Adam replied, sighing. "And she may have just completely ruined this case and allowed a killer to go free."

CHAPTER 19

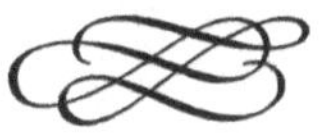

"WELL, *we* have part of the salad," Ruby said.

I glanced over at my ghost who stood at the end of the bed. "What do you mean?"

Adam sat up and stared at me expectantly, waiting for me to finish my conversation.

"When we first found the body, I saw that there were a bunch of seeds on the desk, so I picked them up and dropped them in your purse when no one was looking."

I recalled being in the office and thinking that Ruby couldn't contaminate a crime scene. How wrong I'd been.

"What's she saying?" Adam asked.

I held up a finger, keeping my gaze fixed on my ghost. "They're in my purse?"

"Yes," Ruby said, lacing her hands in front of her and smiling innocently.

"Why in the world would you do that?"

"I don't know," she replied, shrugging. "It seemed like a good idea at the time and then I forgot about it."

I shouldn't be surprised. Ruby had always lived her life in the moment, rarely giving any thought to the consequences of her actions.

"How could you forget that you took something from a crime scene?!" I shouted at her, standing, my hands fisted at my sides.

"Whoa, whoa," Adam said, also getting to his feet. "Calm down, Bernie. Quit screaming. We don't need *anyone* to overhear this conversation."

"Don't you yell at me like that, missy," Ruby said, placing her hands on her hips. "I've been under a lot of stress during this trip. I meant to tell you and I forgot. It's that simple."

"Stress? Stress? You've never known the meaning of the word!"

"Well, I've found it this trip!" Ruby shouted. "It's been awful!"

As my grandmother crumpled to her knees, her whole ghostly body shook. Oh, my word. Could spirits cry?

"Ruby?" I said, lowering myself to the floor

while my anger dissipated and my brow furrowed with concern.

"I don't belong here," she said, meeting my gaze, her face contorted in extreme pain. "I can't go more than fifteen feet away from you. I'm a third wheel even though wheel number two can't see me." She pointed at Adam standing behind me. "You two just got married. You should be busting the mattress springs, but I'm here, hovering around fifteen feet away trying to mind my own business and not being able to."

"Ruby, I—"

"Then I had to watch you come so close to death," she continued. "I've never been so scared, Bernie. I shouldn't be here. I'm a shadow that only you can see. You need to live your life without me hovering over you."

Tears pricked my eyes as I considered all the times I'd thought the same thing while on this trip, and in my life back in Sedona. I'd always felt crippling guilt because I was also one of the lucky ones who got a second chance with a loved one.

I'd never seen my grandmother so upset, so vulnerable. "What... what can we do to make this better for you?"

"I want to go home, Bernie," she whispered. "At least there I can disappear and give you space and freedom. This trip has been awful for everyone. I just want to go home."

As my ghost continued her breakdown, I glanced up at Adam. "We should leave tomorrow. Ruby's… she's really upset."

"Why?"

"Just everything about this trip," I said. "She's feeling like an intruder."

"That's too bad," Adam replied. "What can we do to make her happy?"

"We can go home," Ruby mumbled.

"She wants to leave," I said.

Adam sighed and nodded. "We may as well. The sheriff has said she won't open the church until the crime's been solved. Darla and Jack won't be getting married any time soon. We'll take off after breakfast. What did she say about the crime scene and your purse?"

I debated telling Adam about the seeds. Maybe I'd do a little digging on my own before we left. "Nothing," I said. "It was a misunderstanding."

While I tried to console my inconsolable ghost, I worried what this meant for our future. Ruby had been right: she didn't belong on this plane. But what should I do to help her make the transition to her final resting place?

~

THE NEXT MORNING, I once again rose before everyone in the house and slipped outside with Ruby in tow.

"What are we doing?" she asked as I started the car and pulled away from the curb. "I thought we were heading home."

"We will," I said. "But I want someone to look at those seeds you grabbed from the crime scene."

"Why?"

"Because if we can identify the seeds, then maybe we can find out more about the murderer."

"That's kind of a long shot, Bernie."

"I know I'm grasping at straws, but what if the seeds are what killed him? At least we'd have the murder weapon."

"Good point," she replied with a long sigh.

"And we're going home today," I said, hoping to perk her up.

"Yes."

"Ruby, that's what you wanted," I said. "I thought that would make you happy."

"It does," she said. "But I'm tired of being sort of dead, Bernie. This trip has really made me see that I just don't belong here and I don't understand why I'm stuck in this in-between place."

"To be with me," I said, grinning.

She smiled and ran a cold hand over my arm, causing goosebumps. "I'm lonely, honey. Yes, you can see me, but I'm very much by myself."

"You're kind of being a downer," I whispered.

"Walk a day in my shoes and you'd be depressed as well. I try to keep my spirits up, but it's hard, Bernie. It's really hard. This trip has made me realize how wrong it is for me to be on this plane, tied to my granddaughter like some dog on a leash."

"I don't think of you like that," I said.

"You'd never say it out loud, but I can feel your irritation. Like after your wedding yesterday… you should've had time alone with your husband, not having your old, dead grandma attached to you."

I couldn't argue because I'd had the same thought.

As I pulled into a parking spot in front of Cup of Go, I sighed, hating to see my ghost so upset. "We'll get home later today and get everything sorted out."

We exited the car and went inside. As we waited in line, I studied the menu, pondering whether to go with the fat-free vanilla or hazelnut.

"Can you please get a sugar-filled vanilla latte with a sprinkle of cinnamon?" Ruby asked. "Please? For me? Then tell me all about it?"

I almost began to argue, but then decided to let her live vicariously through me. What could it hurt besides my waistline?

After retrieving my four hundred calorie delicacy, we returned to the car.

"The vanilla tastes amazing with the cinnamon," I said. "A real burst of sugary flavor."

Ruby smiled. "Does the cinnamon remind you of the fall? Like pumpkin pie?"

"A bit," I said, then I took another long drink. "I am getting a sugar and caffeine rush."

"Oh, I loved that feeling," Ruby said. "And the nap that followed a few hours later after the crash wasn't bad, either."

We chatted a few more minutes and headed over to Sage Advice. Another parking spot right in front. Early rising had its benefits.

"Where are the seeds?" I asked, grabbing my purse from the backseat.

"I just tossed them in there. Probably at the bottom."

I pulled out my wallet. "How many of them are there?"

"Three."

I found some old mail I thought I'd thrown away, some lipstick I thought I lost, a couple of ancient, now unwrapped tampons, and a bunch of grocery store receipts. My house was impeccable. My purse, not so much. Finally, I discovered the seeds among a few loose breath mints and some change.

"I'm going to figure out how we know this woman," Ruby said as she pointed at the store, her mood seeming a bit lighter. "And you're smart for bringing those seeds here. She should be able to tell you what they are if she's any good at her job."

"Let's hope so."

I exited the car and noted a sign on the door stating the store didn't open for another hour. We could be on the road by then. "The lights are on," I murmured. "Do you think I should knock?"

"What's the worst that could happen?" Ruby asked, shrugging. "She'll tell you to go away."

I tapped the glass and a moment later, Sam emerged from the back room with a tight smile, obviously irritated at my early morning intrusion.

"Bernie, we don't open for an hour," she said after unlocking the door.

"I see that, but I really, really need your help."

Her brow furrowed in confusion. "You need my help? Can't it wait until after we open?"

"No," I said, shaking my head. "It's urgent."

She sighed and glanced up and down the street. "Okay, come in."

I followed her through the display tables to the counter. A strong scent I didn't recognize filtered out from the back room. "What are you making?" I asked.

"It's a special order for a client—basil and chamomile soap. The girl has acne, so we're trying different combinations to see what clears it up. I have a feeling this is going to be the winner."

"It smells nice."

"Thanks," she replied. "Now, what can I do for you?"

I placed the seeds on the counter.

"What are these?" she asked, pushing her glasses up her nose.

"I was hoping you could tell me what type of plant they are... or will become."

She glanced over the rim of her glasses at me.

"Why? What's this about? And what's the emergency?"

Too many questions. I held my breath, attempting to conjure an evasive answer.

"Just tell her the truth," Ruby said.

"It's about George's murder," I blurted out. "Please don't ask me how I obtained them, but I think one of these could be the murder weapon."

"Oh, really?" she said, arching an eyebrow.

I nodded and prayed she didn't think of me as a lunatic.

"Well, I can say that this right here is a sunflower seed," she said, pointing to the one on the right. "And that one is not a seed, but part of an almond."

"So far, things seem pretty harmless," Ruby said, frowning.

"What about this last one?" I asked.

"I'm not sure about that," Sam replied. She picked it up between her forefinger and thumb and held it up to the light. "Let me take it in back and compare it to some of the pictures in my books. Wait here, please."

My phone buzzed in my pocket, but I didn't bother taking it out. It had to be Adam or one of my friends, and I didn't want to explain what I was doing. Well, at least not until I figured out if me seeking out Sam had been a waste of time.

"You know, I've been thinking about the esteemed sheriff Mallory Richards, and why she didn't have the salad tested right away," Ruby said.

"What about her?" I whispered as I walked toward the front door, glancing around for cameras. The last thing I needed was Sam emerging from the back room and asking me who I was speaking with.

"If the mayor has her in his back pocket, maybe he *is* involved in George's murder. He offs the minister and tells Mallory to tamper with the evidence. She then does her best to screw up the investigation."

I stared at the jars lining the shelves on the wall.

"Think about it, Bernie. Maybe she was the one who was supposed to find George and clean up the salad, but instead, we did."

Okay, a possibly valid point. "Why did she ask Adam and Gunner to help?" I spoke under my breath.

"Because you keep your enemies close. The closer the better."

Talk about a scandal! The mayor killed the

minister and had the sheriff cover it up. Having never met the mayor, I couldn't speak to his character, but I did know his kid was nothing but trouble. Maybe the proverbial apple didn't fall far from the tree.

Ruby snapped her fingers. "I just realized where I know Sam!"

I stared at her expectantly, waiting for an answer.

"But I'm not going to tell you," she said, grinning. "I want to see if you can figure it out. If you can't, I'll give you a few hints."

"Where did you say you got this?" Sam asked, emerging from the back room.

"I didn't," I replied, smiling, hoping she wouldn't press further.

She stared at me long and hard, like a school principal would glare at an unruly child.

"I really believe the less you know, the better," I said.

"Am I going to get in trouble for this?" she asked.

I shook my head. "I promise. This is just for my information."

After mumbling something about having been in enough trouble for three lifetimes, she returned to the back room and came out with an open, hardback book. Laying it out on the counter, she turned so it faced me.

"This seed is a castor bean seed," she said. "They grow indigenously in regions like Ethiopia and some parts of Africa."

I stared at the pictures of the tall, bush like plant with beautiful red flowers and tapped the page. "Where have I seen this before?"

"I've never noticed one around here," Sam said. "But they could grow in this climate with a little TLC. Instead of blooming all year, they'd flower annually."

"Bridezilla's place!" Ruby shouted. "They were at Bridezilla's!"

Tricia Yeats. The pretty, yet deadly, plants had been growing on the side of her house.

"Do you think these could be considered rare in this area?" I asked.

Sam shrugged. "Like I mentioned, I've never seen them growing, and I tend to pay attention to that stuff as I drive by people's homes. I'd notice a castor bean plant. The seeds, like the one you have here, are absolutely deadly."

CHAPTER 20

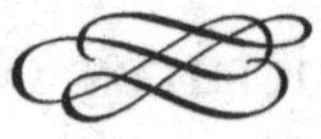

"WE SHOULD GO GRAB ADAM," I said while we pulled away from Sage Advice.

"Tell him to meet you there," Ruby replied. "That seems like the best thing."

After retrieving my phone, I called my husband and relayed what I'd learned. "I saw this particular plant at Tricia Yeats' home," I said. "Since she had an issue with George and has this bush growing at her house which isn't indigenous to this area, I think it has to be her."

"Wow, great work, Bernie," he said. "Give me the address. I'll call the sheriff."

After I hung up, I turned to Ruby and saw a bit of her old spark again. "Cagney and Lacey are on the move!" I said, hoping to excite her again.

"Yes, we are," she beamed. "We're kicking butts, taking names, and solving murders."

Her voice didn't hold the same pizazz it usually did. And she didn't shout at the top of her lungs. My grandmother hadn't been joking when she'd mentioned she was depressed.

"Ruby, everything's going to be okay," I said. "We'll get home and things will go back to normal. You were right. This trip has been awful."

She nodded and turned toward the passenger window.

"So, what's the plan?" I asked, hoping to engage her. "How are we going to nail Tricia?"

"Well, I say you just tell her what you know and watch her reaction."

What the heck? No elaborate schemes? My grandmother was broken! "You'll have my back, though?"

"Of course, Bernie."

Unfortunately, I had my doubts. The Ruby in my vehicle seemed to be a shadow of her former self, and it both saddened and worried me. What if things didn't change when we got home? What if she still felt like an intruder in our house with Adam and me living there? I could only hope the situation would work itself out. No doubt, the trip to Heywood had been horrible, and a reset back in Sedona may be exactly what we needed.

I waited for Adam at the bottom of the driveway where my car couldn't be spotted from the house. A few moments later, he pulled up behind me.

"Where's Gunner?" I asked. "And Sheriff Richards? I thought you were bringing the calvary."

"Gunner, Jezebel, Darla and Jack decided to leave early this morning," he replied. "Richard and Mandy told me when I finally rolled out of bed."

"They left before I did?" I asked.

"Yes."

And I thought we were going to be the bad apples among our friends for wanting to get out of the area. They beat us to it. "And Mal?"

"She's on her way and she's requested we wait for her."

"That's a terrible idea," Ruby said. "What if she's covering for the mayor? Tricia is the mayor's son's girlfriend. She could go in there and then tell us there's nothing to see."

I repeated Ruby's thoughts and Adam nodded. "She's right. I'll just pretend I didn't hear that order. Let's head up to the house."

My ghost sighed. "I'm always right, and it's exhausting."

"I also heard from Sheriff Walker," Adam said. "I gave him the address and he's on his way here."

Ugh. Walker was not one of my favorite people, but my ghost seemed to think he was something quite special. Even the announcement of him arriving at any moment didn't garner a lewd comment or two from her.

When we arrived back at our home, Adam and I would have to have a long talk on what we could do to cheer up Ruby. He'd leased his condo to an older gentleman who sat around all day watching westerns, which thrilled Ned, the ghost, who still had no interest in seeing Ruby. Maybe I'd somehow have to find another spirit for her to socialize with. How I would go about doing that, I wasn't sure. Knock on strangers' doors and see if any entities showed themselves? I'd deal with it later. Confronting a possible murderer was far more important.

"Does Buck live here with her?" Adam asked.

I tried to recall if I'd seen any sign of him when Jezebel and I had visited, and I couldn't remember any. However, I also knew that he didn't reside at his parents' house. That room hadn't recently been lived in. "If he doesn't have a place of his own, he must."

"Let's keep an eye out for him," Adam said. "I don't necessarily believe Tricia's the killer."

"Why not?" Ruby and I asked in unison.

"Buck has the background for it," Adam said, shrugging. "Fighting, a stint in prison, not to mention the shooting at the raft. That kid has some issues."

Violence. It seemed to course through his veins. And maybe that was the issue—it had been built into his DNA.

"You stay here," Adam ordered. "I'll go check things out."

"Wrong answer," Ruby replied.

"No, Adam. I'm going with you." Suddenly, I became very conscious of the fact someone could be hiding behind any of the number of trees around us and we were out in the open. An easy target.

"Bernie, please—"

"Adam, no. I'm going with you," I repeated. "It's dangerous for us to be separated."

He stared at me a long moment, then shook his head and cursed under his breath. "Stay on this side of the driveway until we can see the house. These bushes will provide you the most cover."

He mumbled something about wishing he had a weapon, and I couldn't agree more when the old cabin came into view. The pretty castor bushes caught my eye once again, and it was hard to believe they were so deadly simply because of their beauty.

"We're sitting ducks out here," I whispered, staring at the deck and the open door through the foliage to the house.

"She isn't aware that *you* know she's got the killer plants in her yard," Ruby said. "Just play it cool."

Point taken. And, Tricia probably wouldn't be as threatened by me as she would by Adam. I stepped out in front of him and called, "Tricia?"

"Bernie!" Adam hissed. "What the heck are you doing?"

The old hound dog trotted out of the house and began howling while wagging his tail. Adam came to my side.

"Hey, my old friend!" Ruby yelled, waving at him. "I'm back!"

Tricia came out and placed her hands on her hips, shaking her head. "What do you want?" she called.

"Just to talk to you for a minute," I said. "Can we come up?"

She motioned us up the stairs, and my heart thundered as we climbed them. We found her standing in the doorway as if she were a bouncer blocking our entrance into the club.

"What's up?" she asked. Ruby sat down in front of the dog and began whispering sweet nothings while petting him.

"Have you seen Buck around recently?" Adam asked, his gaze nervously flitting from the doorway and back to her.

Tricia crossed her arms over her chest. "Not since yesterday. Why?"

"Just curious," he replied with a charming smile. "We just wanted to speak to him for a minute."

I didn't believe her. Every bone in my body told me Buck was hiding inside the house.

"Yeah, she's full of crap," Ruby said, standing. She walked over to the door, ghosted through the woman, and peeked inside. I studied the goosebumps as they crawled over Tricia's flesh. "He's here, in the living room," Ruby yelled. "I can see him standing over by the far wall."

I took a deep breath, grabbed Adam's hand and hoped to convey my worry and fear.

"Man, this place needs a good scrubbing," Ruby said as she stepped inside. "Come closer, Bernie. I'm at the end of this stupid leash."

Releasing Adam's palm, I slid a couple of steps toward the door.

"What are you doing?" Tricia asked. "You aren't coming in my house."

"Trust me, you don't want to do that," Ruby called. "But we do have a problem, besides someone not doing their due diligence with a mop. Buck has a bow and arrow set next to him—within arm's reach, Bernie!"

Oh, heck. The idiot was armed. Would he be able to shoot at a human as easily as he'd shot at the raft? Probably. He could've easily missed the raft and hit one of us, which didn't seem to worry him a bit.

"I don't want to come into your house," I said. "Why would you think that I did? Unless you're hiding something in there that you don't want me to see."

As Tricia narrowed her gaze at me, the old hound tried to push past her to get to Ruby. She didn't budge. "There's nothing in there for you to see," she said. "Just me living my life."

"Getting back to the reason for our visit, when

was the last time you saw Buck again?" Adam asked.

"Yesterday."

Adam glanced at the door again. "Does he live here?"

"Well, we *are* engaged," Tricia said. "He spends a lot of time here."

At the far side of the railing, I could see a bit of the castor bean plants peeking over the top. "What are those?" I asked, pointing to the pretty red flowers. "I'd like to get some for my house. Don't you think those would look great out front, Adam?"

"Yes," he grumbled.

I stared expectantly at Tricia. "Do you know what they're called?"

She shook her head, but I saw it in her gaze—she was aware of the plant name and that its seeds were deadly.

"I know what you did," I said, my voice low so Buck couldn't hear me. "You poisoned George."

Adam whispered a curse as Tricia's gaze widened. "How dare you accuse me of such a thing!" she screeched.

"How dare you *do* such a thing?" Ruby said from behind her. "You aren't just a bridezilla. You're nuttier than an almond tree."

"We know what killed George," I said, keeping my gaze firmly directed right above her shoulder. If I saw any movement from Buck, Adam and I would have to make a run for it. "Don't you think it's odd that your house is the only one I've noticed where a plant that's indigenous to Africa grows? It's not like it just sprouted up, Tricia. It was planted and nurtured. By you."

Her cheeks turned the shade of apples as her fists balled at her sides. "I have no idea what you're talking about, but I think you should leave."

"Not until you tell me how you got the castor seeds onto his salad," I replied. "Then I'll be happy to go."

If Buck had heard this exchange, which I had no doubt, then he was in on it. If someone had accused Adam of murder on my front steps, I certainly wouldn't be hiding out inside.

"Did you plant it in the church refrigerator?" I continued. "Maybe brought it to him as a peace offering for being such a little snot about your wedding date?"

"How dare you!" she yelled as she lunged for me and tackled me to the decking. "Do you know who I am?!"

I stared up at Tricia's crazy eyes for a half-second as I tried to catch my breath while Adam shouted and reached for her. All of my self-defense courses finally kicked in and I jammed my palm up into her nose. She screamed and out of the corner of my eye I noticed Buck behind Ruby, raising his bow and arrow. He aimed for Adam's back.

"Get off me!" I yelled, as I punched Tricia in the liver. "Ruby! Behind you! Adam move!"

Adam yanked Tricia upward and tossed her across the deck as if she weighed no more than a pillow, her head slamming against the railing and rendering her unconscious. As the old hound began to howl, Adam helped me to my feet and I noted my grandmother was holding a baseball bat, ready to swing it at Buck. I pushed Adam out of the way and dove on top of him. An arrow whizzed by my head as the crack of the bat meeting Buck's body rang in my ears.

For a second, everything stilled, the only sound being blood rushing through my ears and the dog's cry as he ran into the house.

I stood up slowly as Adam stared at me. Buck lay in the doorway face down.

"Oh, my word!" Ruby screamed as she dropped the bat and ran to the railing. "Bruce! Bruce!"

As I glanced behind me, my breath caught in my throat. Sheriff Bruce Walker lay on the ground with an arrow in his chest.

CHAPTER 21

THE THREE OF us ran down the stairs just as Mallory pulled up. Adam screamed for her to call an ambulance, then pointed to the house. After she radioed in for the paramedics, she ran up the stairway while Adam yelled for her to cuff Buck and Tricia while he attempted to stop Sheriff Walker's bleeding.

"Don't you dare die, you stupid old coot!" Ruby screamed hysterically as she paced, her gaze wide with terror fixed on her former lover.

"What do I need to do to help you?" I asked Adam. Glancing up at the deck, I saw Mallory manhandling both Tricia and Buck. At least she seemed to have everything under control and we could concentrate on helping the sheriff.

A slew of curses fell from Adam's lips. "Check his car for a first aid kit."

I hurried over to the sedan, my hands shaking as I opened the door. After looking in the back-seat, I quickly figured out how to pop the trunk. I ran to the back and found a small first aid kit, then rushed it back to Adam.

"Here," I said, shoving it at him.

"Get some gauze out of there," he muttered.

Ruby sank to her knees by Bruce's head while I opened the white case and handed Adam the gauze. The blood continued to seep from the wound while I laid my fingers on Bruce's wrist and checked for a pulse.

"Should you pull out the arrow?" I asked.

Adam shook his head. "That's the worst thing I could do. Where's the dang ambulance?!"

I listened for sirens, but silence enveloped the area. The birds had become quiet and even the trees seemed to hold their breath as we all waited to discover the fate of Sheriff Walker.

"Don't die, Bruce," Ruby whispered. "At least while you're alive I can still see you. Don't leave me. I'm so sad, and every time I lay eyes on you, it gives me a slice of happiness."

If the man hadn't been bleeding in front of me, I couldn't have been more shocked. Ruby had always said Bruce drove her nuts and their relationship had been tumultuous at best. Had he been the one to steal her heart? And she'd never made anyone aware of it. Instead, she chattered on about how miserable she'd been with him.

Feeling completely useless, I shut my eyes and prayed the feeble pulse beneath my fingertips strengthened while Adam worked and swore. Ruby continued to beg Bruce to live. When I no longer felt a rhythm beneath my fingertips, an icy chill came over me and tears welled in my eyes. No, I'd never liked Sheriff Walker, but I didn't wish him dead, either.

"He's gone," I whispered.

Adam shook his head and attempted CPR as Ruby wailed. I longed to wrap my arms around my ghost and comfort her, but I couldn't even do that. I sat on the ground, defeat rolling through me as the tears cascaded down my face. Both my grandmother and my husband had lost someone and the pain emanating from both almost became a tangible force.

"I'm so sorry," I whispered minutes later when Adam finally gave up on the CPR. He sat down next to me and stared at his blood-covered hands. "You did everything you could."

"Where's the ambulance?" he asked, his voice cracking. "Why did it take so long?"

Ruby stood and began to pace. "I need to get out of here!" she screamed at the sky. Did she mean out of Heywood, or off this plane? As she dropped to her knees and folded herself into a ball and screamed, I didn't know what to do. I sat completely paralyzed by fear and worry.

In the background, I heard Mallory's radio clicking on and off, but I didn't bother to glance up to see how things were going on the deck. If she didn't have two unconscious people under control, she didn't deserve to carry a badge.

"What in the heck is going on here?"

My heart skipped a beat as I gasped, jumped to my feet, and turned. There stood Bruce Walker in his ghostly form with the arrow lodged in his chest, his face contorted in confusion. "Oh, my goodness," I whispered, placing my hand over my mouth.

"What's wrong with you, Bernadette?" he asked. "You look like you've just seen a ghost. And who put this arrow in my chest?"

I tried to laugh, but it came out as a snort and hiccup. This change of events both scared and fascinated me.

Ruby slowly stood. "Bruce?"

His eyes widened as their gazes met. "Ruby? What… you're dead! You've been dead for years!"

Her lips curved in a wide smile. "And so are you, handsome!" She ran to him and they embraced. Ruby delicately maneuvering around the weapon to get a good grip.

I stared slack-jawed at the ghosts.

"What do you mean I'm dead?" Walker asked in a perplexed tone.

Ruby pointed to his body. "You were shot by the little turd on the deck."

Bruce glanced over at his corpse, then back at Ruby. "Wait a minute. You died years ago. What's going on here?"

Suddenly, I felt a significant shift within me, almost as if my organs were rearranging themselves. I leaned over as bile rose in my throat and I realized something momentous was taking place—I didn't understand it, nor could I put a label on it. My breath stuck in my throat as my mind raced to figure it out.

"Are you okay?" Adam asked, standing. "You look sick."

"Bruce is here," I whispered. "He and Ruby are together."

"What?!"

I rose to my full height and placed my finger

over my lips so I could hear the rest of the conversation.

"After I died, I didn't go anywhere. I've been stuck here," Ruby said. "Bernie is the only one who can see me."

"Why?"

"We don't know, handsome," Ruby replied. "It's a mystery and there doesn't seem to be an answer anyone wants to share with us."

"That had to have been tough for you," Bruce said. "My gem of a gal, Ruby, goes from always being the center of attention to no one hearing her. I can't imagine how much that hurt."

"It did, Bruce. I love Bernie with all my heart, but this has not been fun. At first, I was thrilled to have someone to talk to, and we did have some good times, but lately… it's been hard keeping my chin up."

"Well, I see you just fine," Bruce said, running his hand over her cheek. "And I like that I can. I always knew how to make you happy, didn't I?"

"I've missed you so much," Ruby said, her voice the sincerest I'd ever heard. "I know we had our issues, but I did love you, even when you were the biggest killjoy I'd ever met."

"You only thought that because you like to break the laws I'm supposed to uphold."

"*Were* supposed to uphold. You're dead now. Laws don't matter anymore."

He glanced around. "I'm not sure about this. I see my body over there, but I can't believe I bit the big one. I don't know what to do next."

"I'll show you the ropes, cowboy," Ruby replied. "There's not much to it. But things just got a whole lot better for me."

"Adam, can I talk to you for a minute?" Mallory asked, completely unaware of the reunion taking place. I'd been so focused on Ruby, I hadn't heard her approach.

"Um… yeah." He glanced at me, concern shining in his gaze. I was too stunned to assure him I wouldn't pass out at any moment. Anyway, it would've been a lie.

As they stepped away, the ambulance arrived.

"A little too late, losers!" Ruby yelled, linking her arms through the sheriff's. "He's all mine now!"

While Adam and Mallory spoke to the EMT's I stared at Ruby and Bruce. My ghost beamed with happiness while dread filled me. What in the world was I going to do with them? I could barely handle Ruby alone, but throw in Bruce? She'd once described their relationship as oil and water. I didn't want the drama in my life. Things seemed to be going along smoothly at the present mo-ment, but what would happen when Ruby's antics became too much and they argued, like she and Ned often did?

Ruby sauntered over, grinning from ear to ear. "You feel it too, don't you?"

"I… I don't know." The uneasy clench in my chest continued to grow, but I couldn't identify it.

"It's time," Ruby said.

"T-time for what?"

"For me to go."

My head began to spin and I leaned over and placed my hands on my knees. "Go where, Ruby?"

"Away."

And just like that, I gasped as if she'd punched me in the gut. I swallowed past the bile and stood to my full height. Leaving me? The idea hurt worse than managing her and Bruce's fights. "W-what do you mean? You can't leave me. You can't go fifteen feet away from me. The tether… re-member? We're joined together."

"We *were* joined together," Ruby said gently. "But not anymore. That weird feeling inside of you? It's the leash breaking."

Tears welled in my eyes as I realized she was saying goodbye. "How do you know?"

"I just do," she said, her brow creased and her

lips set in a fine line. I'd never seen her so serious. "I hear it in the wind and feel it deep inside me. It's happening, and it's time for me to go."

No. *This couldn't be happening.*

"But why?" I asked, crossing my arms over my chest. I realized I probably appeared defiant, but I really was trying to comfort myself… attempting to hold myself together. "Why now?"

"We aren't aware of all the rules, Bernie. But I can tell you this: I know in the deepest depths of my soul that I was stuck here waiting for Bruce."

"How… how do you know that?"

"I just do," she said, shrugging. "You feel it as well. You look like you're going to toss your cookies all over me. It's hard, but it's happening."

The ache in my chest was so strong, I wondered if my heart would splinter apart.

"You can't leave me," I whispered, wiping my nose.

"I have to," Ruby said. "I've got my other half here with me now, and it's time for you and Adam to move forward without me so you can discover if he's the one for you. You don't need me around all the time."

"Where… where will you go?"

Bruce walked over and settled his arm around her. "Well, heaven doesn't want her, and the folks in hell are afraid of her, so I figure we'll be around."

Despite my utter sorrow, I smiled.

"We'll be close," Ruby said, running a hand over my arm. "If you need me, just shout, and I'll come running."

As they turned, held hands, and walked down the driveway, I sank to my knees and bawled like a baby. My chest heaved as I tried to catch my breath. Paramedics circled me, but I waved them away. They couldn't fix what had broken me.

The first time Ruby had died, I'd lost touch with her, but it still hurt. I'd been so grateful when I'd been struck by lightning and I was able to see her once again. Yes, she drove me crazy at times, but I loved her fiercely and appreciated the second chance. With her leaving me again, the wound of loss was fresh and devastating.

I'd asked for this… for time alone with Adam. And now that I had what I'd wished for, I couldn't imagine the next ten minutes without Ruby around, let alone weeks, months, or years.

"I love you, Ruby!" I called out. Ruby turned, smiled, and blew me a kiss, then they vanished.

"Miss?" one paramedic said, leaning over me. "Who are you talking to?"

"It's okay," Adam replied, placing his hand on

my back. "She's really upset over the sheriff's death. I'll take it from here."

As he helped me stand and led me over to the car, I tried to regain my wits and ignore the well of never-ending emptiness consuming me. He turned to me once we were seated inside. "What the heck is going on, Bernie?"

Closing my eyes, I leaned my head back against the headrest. "She's gone, Adam. Ruby's gone."

EPILOGUE

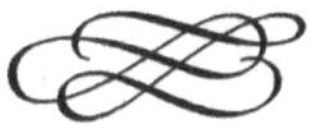

BUCK AND TRICIA eventually confessed to George's murder and Buck admitted to shooting at our raft. It had been purely accidental we were the ones riding in it. He had been trying to hurt the other rafting business so he could sweep in and brand himself the "safe" rafting company.

Tricia had brought George the salad as a peace offering for the tantrum she'd thrown about her wedding date, claiming she'd grown all the vegetables herself. George, being the godly man he was, took the gift with gratitude and accepted her apology. She claimed she watched him eat it and left as he began to have a reaction to the castor seeds. Somehow, she and Buck had convinced themselves the law didn't apply to them because of Buck's father being the mayor. Using his influence, he'd been able to convince a judge to lower Buck's prior prison time. I concluded that Tricia and Buck were little people who wanted to be important but didn't want to work to achieve that status.

My marriage continued to flourish and grow. Adam actually threw in his hat to become the sheriff but was beaten out by another man in the department. Although I was disappointed for him, I also appreciated he could spend more time with me. The bed and breakfast had its good and bad months, depending on the season. However, I didn't worry as much about money because we had Adam's steady salary coming in.

Darla and Jack finally got married in a small ceremony next to a stream in Sedona. It had been beautiful with the sound of water trickling by, the red rocks as a backdrop, and plenty of trees to provide shade. Of course, everyone was shocked Adam and I had secretly tied the knot, and Darla was furious we'd been so sneaky. Her anger subsided when I mentioned we were going to have a proper ceremony as well and she'd be catering it.

As for Ruby, I didn't directly see or hear from her for months. I tried calling out to her a few times to see if she'd come, but I was met with deafening silence. Sometimes, at night, I'd wake to the sound of her and Bruce's laughter downstairs, but if I ventured down to catch them, they'd be gone. Some mornings I woke up to little pranks like the coffee pot being hidden or my hairbrush missing, neither of which I found amusing—especially the missing coffee pot. Cruelty, I say.

Elvira often stared at something that wasn't there, so I knew Ruby was present. She just wasn't showing herself.

I'd come to terms with my loss and missed my ghost terribly. However, I did find a lot of joy in the little quiet moments Adam and I shared... moments that never would've happened if Ruby had been present.

There was only one thing I hadn't made peace with—and admittedly, it was a bit silly.

Ruby had said she knew from where she recognized Sam from the herbal shop, Sage Advice, in Heywood.

But she never told me, and sometimes when I couldn't sleep, I lay in bed, staring at the ceiling and trying to place Sam's face. Yes, she was familiar to me as well... but for the life of me, I couldn't figure out why.

· · ·

To FIND out who Sam is, please grab the anthology, Mysteries, MidSummer Sun and Murders. You'll get 20 brand new summer themed cozies mysteries for a mere .99, and it is the beginning of a new series for me: the Heywood Herbalist Cozy Mysteries featuring the mysterious Sam, the small, idyllic town of Heywood, and its cast of questionable characters.

ALSO BY CARLY WINTER

Sedona Spirt Mysteries

Bernie and the ghost of her dead grandmother find themselves in the middle of various murder investigations. Danger and hilarity ensues as the crazy duo follow the clues to discover the killers.

The Tri-Town Murders

Complete Series

Follow newspaper reporter Tilly and her group of fun, quirky friends as they solve murders in a fictional, small town in California.

News and Nectarines

News and Nachos

News and Nutmeg

News and Noodles

Killer Skies Mysteries

Set in 1965, join Patty Briggs, stewardess extraordinaire, as she flies the skies and solves murders with the help of her friends… and one cute FBI agent!

ABOUT THE AUTHOR

Carly Winter is the pen name for a USA Today best-selling and award-winning romance author.

When not writing, she enjoys spending time with her family, reading and enjoying the fantastic Arizona weather (except summer - she doesn't like summer). She does like dogs, wine and chocolate and wishes Christmas happened twice a year.

For more information on her books and to join her cozy mystery author report, please visit:
CarlyWinterCozyMysteries.com

Follow her on:
BookBub
Books2Read
Goodreads

www.ingramcontent.com/pod-product-compliance
Lightning Source LLC
Chambersburg PA
CBHW011211190726
48288CB00013B/3400